The Sorcerer's Dau

A Yadu girl and two young
from the sorcerers.

Sarba has good reason ~~to hate and fear the conquered~~
Xerappans. She is proud when her father, the fearsome Yadu
High Sorcerer, sends her into Xerappo to investigate. Perhaps
at last she will earn his love. But her life is turned upside down
by the most ordinary of creatures – a sparrow.

The young sorcerer Tekran is one of that mission. What he
finds there challenges his vows to defend his country.

Soon Sarba and Tekran are fleeing on camels too. The
hunters have become the hunted. Can the power of Sarba's
Ring and Tekran's sorcery save them now?

Fay Sampson is the author of many books for children,
teenagers and adults, including the popular Pangur Bán
series. She lives with her husband in a centuries-old cottage
overlooking Dartmoor, from which she enjoys walking the
moors and coast. As well as writing stories of her own, she
loves discovering the story of her ancestors' lives.

Also by Fay Sampson:
The Sorcerer's Trap
Pangur Bán, the White Cat
Finnglas of the Horses
Finnglas and the Stones of Choosing
Shape-Shifter: the Naming of Pangur Bán
The Serpent of Senargad
The White Horse is Running
The Christmas Blizzard
THEM

To Alex

The Sorcerer's Daughter

FAY SAMPSON

LI♥N
CHILDREN'S

Text copyright © 2007 Fay Sampson

The moral rights of the author
have been asserted

A Lion Children's Book
an imprint of
Lion Hudson plc
Wilkinson House, Jordan Hill Road,
Oxford OX2 8DR, England
www.lionhudson.com
ISBN: 978 0 7459 6072 2

First edition 2007
1 3 5 7 9 10 8 6 4 2 0

A catalogue record for this book is available
from the British Library

Typeset in 10/13.5 ITC Garamond Bk BT
Printed and bound in Great Britain
by Cox and Wyman Ltd, Reading

The text paper used in this book has been made from wood
independently certified as having come from sustainable forests.

Chapter One

Sarba sneaked a proud glance down the folds of her white robe. Two crimson bands circled above the hem, where last week there had been only one. She had taken her second-year vows. She was fifteen.

Sarba Cozuman was a Ring-Holder of the temple on Mount Femarrat. It would have been surprising if she had not been. She was, after all, the High Sorcerer's only child, even though he had banished her from his home ten years ago.

Around her, the courtyard of Lord Cozuman's house, where she had not been since she was a child, was crowded. Guests were seated at tables in the summer evening, enjoying food and wine at her cousin's eve-of-betrothal party.

Suddenly, they were starting to their feet. There was a commotion: cries of alarm, gasps of wonder.

Sarba's eyes shot up. The Sorcerer Guard, resplendent in white dress uniforms, instead of their workaday crimson tunics and trousers, were reaching for their spell-rods. Other Ring-Holders, wearing robes like Sarba's, were craning forward. Civilian guests in gauzy dresses of green and rose and lavender were backing away. Through the excited throng, a path was opening up.

Pacing towards her, its jewelled collar glittering in the lamplight, came a magnificent leopard with green eyes. Sarba stared, fascinated, at the creature. She had never seen a leopard, on Mount Femarrat or anywhere else. There were none in the land of Yadu.

Was this a surprise her father, the High Sorcerer, or the bridegroom, Digonez, had devised to impress the guests?

The leopard was pacing closer and closer. Guests were falling back to form a corridor of curious faces. Sarba's eyes moved on past the leopard.

The blood left her face. A shudder ran through her from head to foot. It was not the big cat, almost within reach now, which terrified her, but the boy behind it, holding its leash.

He was totally unlike any of the Children of Yadu surrounding him. All of them, like Sarba herself, were tall, slender, with straight, blond hair. This boy was short, broad-shouldered, dark brows scowling under the thatch of black curls. He wore baggy trousers and a smock embroidered with outlandish designs. In spite of the fact that there were guards on either side of him, the sight of him made Sarba sick with fear.

She felt her friend Kelith tugging at her elbow. 'Sarba, you idiot, move out of the way!'

She let herself be pulled back into the crowd. The leopard's green eyes shone through the patch of twilight between the lamps. It passed so close she could have put out a hand to touch its speckled black-and-gold coat.

Now she did want to back away, but the press of the crowd behind her would not allow her to. She could not retreat far enough from the boy following. He came too close. She could smell his sweat, see the frown of his black brows, the grim set of his mouth. He was about her age.

Then the unbearable moment was over. He and his sorcerer guards were past her.

Sarba let out her breath in a shaky gasp that was almost a sob. 'A Xerappan *here?* On Mount Femarrat itself?'

She watched in disbelief as the foreign boy and his leopard made their way to where the High Sorcerer stood waiting in his white robe, with the figure of her cousin Digonez beside

6

him, handsome in his white dress uniform. The habitual severe lines of Lord Cozuman's face betrayed no sign of emotion as the Xerappan approached him. Digonez, at least, looked anxious as he murmured something to the High Sorcerer. A little to one side of them was the slender Alalia Yekhavu, the girl Digonez was to be betrothed to in the morning, with her sorcerer brother Balgo beside her. She looked as pale as a moth in her lemon-yellow dress.

Kelith let go of Sarba's arm. 'What's the matter with you? You've gone as white as your robe. What's so strange about a Xerappan servant, after all? The bride's from a Yadu colony over the border in Xerappo. They're saying she'll be driven to her betrothal tomorrow in a chariot drawn by leopards. That'll be a sight to remember, won't it?'

'But why have they let him in? A Xerappan in my father's house!'

Kelith stared at her for a moment. Then her hand flew to her mouth. 'Oh, Sarba, I'm sorry! I never thought. Your mother...'

Sarba turned and plunged away from her into the crowd.

She was fighting frantically against the tide of bodies. Everyone else was pressing forward to see this Xerappan display his leopard to the High Sorcerer and his guests. Why had her father invited him here? There must be a reason. Everything Lord Cozuman did was for the good of Yadu, to keep the country safe from these murderous rebels. So why let one of those hated foreigners inside the magical Fence, which guarded the sacred mountain of Femarrat? She could not bear the thought, not after what had happened ten years ago...

She had left the crowd and the lamplight behind. She was a little girl again, hurt and crying, running across this courtyard to the safety of her home and her mother...

She pulled up short. The door to the house was open, but guarded.

One of the sentries moved to challenge her, but the other put a restraining hand on his arm.

'That's his daughter,' he muttered.

Reluctantly, the first sorcerer let her pass.

Even as she entered the cool, dim corridor, a wave of anger swept over Sarba. *They shouldn't have let me in. They shouldn't let anyone in here without tonight's password, and I don't know it. It's not enough that I'm the High Sorcerer's daughter, when I haven't set foot in this house for ten years. Not since...*

It was too painful to go on. She must not let herself remember that day on the beach.

Half-blinded with tears at the memories which threatened to choke her, she stumbled on down the corridor. This house was only half-remembered. She opened the door of the living room. She had been five years old when she last saw it. It seemed smaller now. Certainly, it was more severely furnished. Gone were the vases of flowers she recalled, the scent of oleander blossom, the colourful rugs where she and her mother had played with her toys. The High Sorcerer had swept away all reminders of the love and laughter that used to be in this house. There was a bare, polished red floor, a few pieces of severe furniture. Nothing soft or frivolous remained.

A hiccuping sob threatened to undo her. She gripped her fists, so that the nails dug into her palms. She must not cry. She must keep hold of her anger. She had vowed her life, as her father had, to protect Yadu, to make sure that the hated Xerappans never, ever took one foothold of this land back from them.

She turned away from the room, dashing the treacherous tears from her eyes. How could she let her father know how well she understood his severity, how much she wanted to share his work of protecting Yadu? He never spoke to her now. She had been swept away with those rugs and cushions and flowers, sent to the school in the township of Mount Femarrat. She was a Ring-Holder now, vowed to a life of service in Femarrat's temple. She was probably no more to Lord Cozuman than any other Ring-Holder. This was not her home. She had no right to be here.

Still she walked on. She felt a vibration under her feet. A growing hum was assailing her ears. She must be very close now to the Control Room, in the depths of the mountain. Here, night and day, shifts of sorcerers kept the Power going. Their strength and skill maintained the shimmering Fences around Mount Femarrat and along the border between Yadu and Xerappo. Their magic armed every spell-rod which the sorcerers carried on their belts. Magic was no light thing. It took enormous effort to sustain the spells. It was this Power she called down daily in the flame of the temple on the summit, to serve the sorcerers. The warmth of pride comforted her a little.

'Who goes there? Password?'

She almost screamed. She had not noticed the figure in the shadows at the end of the corridor.

'I... I...' She had no excuse. She had no business here. She was no longer the High Sorcerer's little daughter, playing hide-and-seek with her mother. She was just a second-year Ring-Holder, no more important than any other guest at this betrothal-eve party. She was not authorized to enter the house.

The sorcerer strode towards her. She should be grateful he had not used his spell-rod to stun her. In the dim light, she made out that he was wearing his everyday crimson tunic and trousers, not the white dress uniform of the party guests. He must have been on duty in the Control Room below.

'Sarba! What are you doing here?'

'Tekran!' A wave of relief engulfed her. Tekran was only two years older than her, one of the group of young sorcerers and Ring-Holders who would meet in the courtyard of the inn for cool drinks and chatter after the day's work was over.

'Look, I'm sorry. I know I shouldn't be here. I was just... curious... It's been so long.'

'You've never been back here since then?' She heard the compassion in his voice. He knew her story.

'No. I've never been back. I expect he couldn't bear to see me... afterwards. I'm whole and well, while she...'

Close to, she read sympathy in his eyes as he looked down at her from under those oddly tufted brows. It struck her that Tekran was different from any of the other sorcerers. It had never occurred to her before. Even the youngest of them, her friends, would have ejected her forcefully and reported her to their superiors for trespassing in the High Sorcerer's house. They would have been right; it was their duty. She was committing a grave breach of security.

The realization that Tekran would not report her both relieved and alarmed her. Could he be trusted to guard the land of Yadu? Did he value her friendship more?

Tekran gave an uneasy laugh. 'I'm sorry, but it's hard for the rest of us to imagine Lord Cozuman was ever a family man. We're all terrified of him.'

'As long as the Xerappans are terrified of him, that's all that matters.'

'You still hate them so much?'

'Of course. Don't you? There's one out in the courtyard now, with a leopard. I can't understand why they let him in.'

'It's to do with your cousin's betrothal tomorrow. Balgo was telling me. You remember Balgo, who passed out of Sorcerer School last year? The bride's his sister. Balgo's thrilled to bits that he's standing in for his father at the ceremony.'

'That doesn't explain what a Xerappan's doing here.'

'Balgo's family are from a Yadu colony in Xerappo, where they use lions and leopards instead of horses. His sister must have brought her driver with them.'

'We should never have let a Xerappan set foot on Mount Femarrat. It's sacred.'

'To us. And to them, too, before we came.'

'It's ours now.'

'No doubt about that. Shall I see you out?'

'You ought to report those sentries for letting me in.'

And report me, she thought, but did not say.

'Wouldn't that be a bit harsh? You must have charmed them.'

'It shouldn't be enough that I'm Lord Cozuman's daughter. I could still be a traitor.'

'Somehow, I can't imagine that,' he chuckled as he took her arm.

'How can you know? How do any of us know whom we can trust?'

His hand was warm on her skin.

Should I trust Tekran?

Light dazzled her at the door. An eerie green swept down on the party-goers, changing their upturned faces to ones disturbingly inhuman. Out of the green grew contorted features, leering back at the humans. Shrieks swiftly gave way to sighs of rapture. Menacing crones were replaced by swans who rained rubies out of a sapphire sea.

'Witch-light!' laughed Tekran, applauding. 'Lord Cozuman's not going to be outdone by a Xerappan leopard.'

He turned back to the Control Room and left her. Sarba felt the loss of his hand on her arm.

She edged her way into the crowd, searching for her friend Kelith. A voice halted her.

'Where is Alalia?'

Lord Cozuman's cold voice was so close, she thought for a moment the question was addressed to her. It cut through the laughter of his sorcerers and the astonished cries of the guests.

Sarba's heart seemed to stop. It was years since she had been this close to her father, in this house. Would he notice her?

The High Sorcerer stood taller than was common, even for a Yadu man. His spare figure was clad in a white robe bordered with crimson, not unlike her own. Thin hair, iron-grey now, was combed back over his head, as if flattened by rain. The eyes were cold, grey, directed at the broad-shouldered young officer at his side.

Lieutenant Digonez Cozuman, the bridegroom-to-be, cut a fine figure in his white uniform with crimson epaulettes. This was his night. This party was to honour him and Alalia, who would be betrothed to him tomorrow. Just now, his face was dark with anger.

'She said she was cold. She went to get her cloak. I've lost sight of her.'

'Don't worry. I'll soon find her for you.' The tone of Lord Cozuman's voice was far less reassuring than his words.

His hand drew a little white-and-gold spell-rod from his sleeve. He waved it just once. Sapphire sea and white swans were instantly transformed into a ring of flames. Guests, who had been laughing as they surged forward to catch the falling rubies, screamed now and backed away.

Even Sarba gasped, as out of the flames grew scarlet goblins. Their hideous faces were forming a ring, advancing, closing in.

Then Sarba saw Alalia in their lurid light. She was near the back of the crowd. The girl from the colonies was beautifully dressed for her betrothal-eve. Her straight silvery-blonde hair had been curled into waves and ringlets, piled up on her head and cascading down her back. The fluted yellow dress in

12

which she had arrived was hidden now by a cloak of soft grey feathers. But it could not disguise her. Her face was terrified as the goblins reared up over her.

'That's a bit cruel, isn't it? At her betrothal party?' Kelith was at Sarba's elbow again. 'I know Digonez is your cousin, but *I* wouldn't marry him. He's a bully.'

'Witch-light isn't serious magic, like they do in the Control Room. You know those goblins aren't real,' Sarba said through stiff lips.

'*She* doesn't know that, though, does she?'

Sarba was not listening. She was staring past Alalia. On the far side of the Yadu girl was that figure again: the squat, dark Xerappan boy. At his feet crouched his leopard, its dappled coat almost indistinguishable in the shadows, save for the gleam of its green eyes. His head was close to Alalia's fair one. As the red light caught them, he jerked away.

Sarba shuddered, but not at the leopard. The sight of any Xerappan made her want to vomit. She could never forgive them.

Why was this Yadu bride there, on the outskirts of the crowd, whispering to her Xerappan leopard-driver, instead of at the side of the sorcerer who was to be her husband? How could a girl who looked so like Sarba herself stand that close to him?

As the light from the ring of fire demons intensified, people were backing away from Alalia. The Xerappan leopard boy was dragged from her side. Sarba saw with relief that there were guards holding him.

Alalia stood alone, her pale face lit by scarlet flames. Clawed hands tugged at her carefully arranged hair. Goblin fingers snatched her cloak from her. She screamed as she was swept up over the heads of the guests and rushed through the air towards Lord Cozuman and Digonez. She was dumped unceremoniously at her fiancé's feet.

'That *was* strong magic,' Sarba murmured, 'but it only worked because she believed in it.'

'Now you see why I'd never marry Digonez,' Kelith said. 'What a way to treat her!'

'She's not a Ring-Holder. She won't remember it. You know how a witch-light show always ends.'

Even as she spoke, the faces of the fire demons were softening. Writhing bodies were thinning into flower stems, talons lengthening into slender leaves. The courtyard had become a sea of scarlet poppies. And with them, the mood changed. At a lift of Cozuman's spell-rod, the looks of terror on the faces of the uninitiated guests smoothed into a drowsy contentment. People began to drift towards the gate, arms round each other, telling their companions what a wonderful party it had been. Only the beautiful things would remain in their memories. Nothing ugly, nothing cruel.

Except... As the crowd thinned, Sarba caught sight of the Xerappan again. His face was not like the others. It was alert, angry. A sudden fear chilled her. *The magic isn't working on him. Why not?*

Her eyes flew back to Alalia. She was leaning on Digonez's shoulder, smiling now, as if nothing bad had happened, as if he and Lord Cozuman had not just humiliated her. But even as Sarba watched, a little frown of puzzlement crossed the girl's face. She seemed to be struggling to remember something.

Sarba started. There was another Xerappan following Alalia towards the gate: a girl this time. A smaller version of the black-browed boy with the leopard. It was probably Alalia's maid, from the colony. And her face, too, was awake, indignant.

Standing there, in the courtyard of the High Sorcerer's house, with the Control Room that guarded the whole of Yadu under her feet, on sacred Mount Femarrat itself, Sarba knew the chill certainty that something was terribly wrong.

The magic of the High Sorcerer was not absolute. The Xerappans could break it.

Chapter Two

Dawn was paling the sky as Sarba and Kelith mounted the last steps to the summit. The baskets they carried were heavy, for all the delicacy of their contents. Sarba's was heaped with trails of pink and purple bougainvillaea, still sprinkled with dew. Kelith's bore sweetly scented horns of frangipani and the more delicately perfumed white mimosa. In front of and behind them, more Ring-Holders were similarly burdened. There were girls with a single ring on their skirts, older women with many. Hania, their leader today, in her thirties, had a hooped skirt which showed her to be a Six-Ring-Holder. All were as slender and fair as Sarba herself. On the left wrist of each of them, a carnelian bracelet glowed reddish yellow in the uncertain light of early morning.

The steep steps were ice-green, smooth and slippery, as if frozen, belying the heat which would soon beat down on them. Even as the party toiled towards the summit, a horn sounded. The sun rose, turning the bare slopes of Mount Femarrat to blinding white.

Sarba stopped and looked upwards, shading her eyes. From the black pillars of the temple, a column of fire leaped between earth and sky. Everyone put down their baskets and joined hands. Their eyes smiled kinship at each other. All over this land, the Children of Yadu were one.

They watched the fire sink and settle into a steady flame, growing paler as the sunlight strengthened.

Sarba felt the comfort of relief as she picked up her flowers.

The daily ritual had been performed. Twenty-four more Ring-Holders in white and four sorcerers in red were coming down the steps towards her. They had made the Morning Circle to call down the flame once more. Every noon and sunset, the flame would be renewed. Power would flow in the Control Room in the heart of the mountain. The land of Yadu was safe for another day.

Is it?

Into her mind crawled the fear which had gripped her at the party last night. The angry eyes of those Xerappans.

She and Kelith stood aside to let those descending pass. They were glad of the excuse to rest. The climb was long, the steps high.

'You remember the witch-light yesterday evening?' she said in a low voice. 'There were two Xerappans who didn't fall under the High Sorcerer's spell of forgetfulness: that boy with the leopard, and a girl. I think she was Alalia's maid. You could see it in their faces. They remembered it all.'

'What's the problem?' Kelith shrugged. 'So much the better if they remember the witches and the demons. That ought to scare them off any thoughts of rebellion. I bet your father meant them to remember.'

'I never thought of that.'

They climbed again, the last ascent to the summit.

The natural peak of Femarrat had been hacked away when the Children of Yadu took the land from the Xerappans. The summit was now a platform of dazzling white. It was circled by black pillars, linked overhead to form a ring of shade. The centre stood open to the sky. At this early hour, the sun threw barred shadows from the pillars across it.

Sarba felt the constriction of her heart at the sacred things crossed by those shadows: the massive rectangular block of red jasper; the copper basin, from which rose the column of shimmering flame. This was her task for the rest of her life as

17

a Ring-Holder, to guard this flame, to protect her country.

She looked around her, through the pillars. Colour was flooding back into the world. The emerald green of farmland and palm trees, the sapphire-and-silver dance of the sea, the far purple of the hills which separated Yadu from Xerappo. It was from a colony over those hills that Alalia Yekhavu had come, with her mother and brother and friends and their Xerappan servants, in chariots and carts drawn by leopards and lions.

'Wake up, Sarba,' Hania was scolding. 'We haven't got all morning. I want every one of these flowers in place before the betrothal procession leaves the township.'

The girls set to work. Nimble fingers twined strands of bougainvillaea and mimosa round the black pillars. Frangipani and oleander were heaped at the foot of the altar. They strewed rose petals to make a pink carpet, over which Alalia would walk from her chariot to the Stone, where she would stand at Digonez's side to make her vows. Not for her the steep climb by the steps. A longer, gentler road curved round the mountain, joined by another from the High Sorcerer's house.

The temple was ready, but only just.

'They're on their way!' cried Hania.

From Lord Cozuman's house halfway up the mountain, horsemen were setting out. Sarba's heart beat faster. Her father was riding a black mount, Digonez a white, attended by more sorcerers. Ring-Holders, led by their chief Letizal, and guests in more colourful dress, were approaching along the winding township road. The platform of the temple began to fill.

As so often in her ceremonial duties this past year, she felt her breath stifled in her throat as her father strode into the Circle. White-and-crimson robes, in a temple of white and red and black. Today's profusion of multicoloured flowers looked suddenly out of place beside his severity. Would he recognize her? She knew he would not acknowledge her if he did. Digonez was beside him, handsome again in his white uniform, his head arrogantly high. One day, she knew, he meant to be High Sorcerer himself.

'Her chariot's coming!' Kelith whispered, digging her elbow into Sarba's ribs.

Two leopards crested the rise. They made an alarming sight in a country where donkeys and bullocks were draught animals, and the finer people rode horses. But the passenger in this chariot was not Alalia. A plump woman, in a cloth-of-gold dress, fantastically fringed and tasselled with purple, was helped down. Her face beamed under elaborately curled piles of hair, shaded by a blue-and-gold parasol.

Kelith giggled. 'Her mama. What an embarrassment!'

Emania Yekhavu was led to a place of honour. She looked around, as if expecting to find a seat. There was none. There was a starkness in this temple. All that mattered were the Stone and the flame.

'Funny Alalia's father hasn't come to give her away, for such an important betrothal as this,' Sarba murmured.

'Didn't you hear there were rumours of a Xerappan uprising out there? Her father's governor of the colony. He had to stay. That's why Balgo's giving her away.'

Sarba pictured the rather self-important young man who sometimes shared a drink at Mount Femarrat's inn last year with Tekran, Kelith and herself.

'He'll enjoy that, won't he? He's only a probationer sorcerer, but it'll make him look almost as important as Digonez.'

A larger, flower-decked chariot drawn by lions deposited the bridesmaids, all tall, fair Yadu girls from the colony. Now, only the bride-to-be was needed.

The High Sorcerer, the Chief Ring-Holder, the bridegroom, the guests waited.

The sun climbed higher.

Alalia did not come.

Lord Cozuman turned to Digonez. His voice, though not raised, cut across the restive muttering of the guests.

'Where's the girl?'

'Balgo's bringing her. They'll be here any moment.'

'Balgo Yekhavu? He's hardly finished his first year as a sorcerer. Who does he think he is, to keep the High Sorcerer waiting?'

'I can't explain it, sir.' In desperation, the lieutenant strode across to Emania Yekhavu. 'I expected your daughter before this. Is this the sort of manners you have in the colonies? Do you mean to insult Lord Cozuman?'

The plump woman bridled. 'I'm sure I don't know what the matter is. She was dressed and ready before I left. Perhaps their chariot took a wrong turning.'

'There is no other road up this mountain.'

'I wouldn't put anything past a Xerappan driver. You wouldn't believe how stupid they can be.'

'The leopard boy?'

'But Balgo's with them. He won't stand for any nonsense. He's a qualified sorcerer now, you know.'

'He's still a probationer.'

Digonez spun on his heel. Sarba saw the rage in his face as he returned to the Stone.

He never reached it. The howl of a siren split the silence. Echoes were flung back from bare rock. Gulls rose screeching into the air.

Shock waves galvanized the crowd. Sorcerers whipped their spell-rods from their belts. Sarba and Kelith stared at each other in horror.

Next moment, bolts of fire arced across the sky to explode in the sea.

'Someone's trying to breach the Fence,' thundered Cozuman. 'Seize them!'

Digonez leaped for the steps. In moments, the summit had emptied of sorcerers. Lord Cozuman himself was mounting his black horse, galloping back to the Control Room.

Emania Yekhavu collapsed in tears.

Sarba's heart was thudding so hard, she thought it would break her ribs. What had happened? Her eyes were fixed on the flame in the copper basin. It was almost transparent as the sun beat down on it. Did she only imagine that it was still burning?

She screwed up her eyes against the light. Into the darkness behind her lids came a picture of the fair Alalia whispering to the dark Xerappan boy.

Chapter Three

Those who were not involved in the search were confined to the township.

Kelith rejoined Sarba at the hostel, panting with excitement and fear. 'I saw Tekran for a few moments. They've found a gate open from a tunnel to the beach. The spells hit there, but there's no sign of bodies. He thinks only Balgo could have opened the gate.'

'Balgo was our *friend*! He was here on Mount Femarrat with us last year.' There was an intensity of disbelief in Sarba's voice. 'How could he betray us?'

'Perhaps his sister persuaded him. Maybe she finally got cold feet about marrying Digonez.'

'Or that Xerappan kidnapped her and forced Balgo to open the gate.'

Kelith laughed uneasily. 'How could he do that? A Xerappan servant, against a Yadu sorcerer?'

'I can't explain it, but I warned you this morning. I think they have some power we don't know about.'

Kelith's hand closed over hers, comforting. 'Don't worry. We're safe here. What they did to your mother and those others won't ever happen again. Your father will see to that.'

Even as she spoke, the mountain shuddered. The walls of the hostel shook. The two girls clutched each other, with scared eyes.

'What was *that*? Is someone attacking Mount Femarrat?'

The blood left Sarba's face. 'I'm afraid, Kelith. Is nowhere safe?'

The pool in the temple rocked. Points of light, from torches around the far walls, danced wildly on the black water at the centre. Gamatea, its Guardian, gasped and ran to it.

She bent over the surface. As the waves subsided, she saw the image of her own face. Tawny gold skin looked strangely lighter in the gloom. Her hair was lost in the dark ripples. Bright, bird-like eyes stared back at her, their blue hardly distinguishable here from black. Her reflection looked pure Xerappan.

The image of herself sank beneath the surface. Other scenes rose in its place. The Guardian gasped. Her eyes, whose reflection she could no longer see, widened in horror.

'The chamber under Mount Femarrat! They would destroy that, in revenge?'

The woman guarding the temple door called out in alarm, 'Is something wrong, madam? Shall I call for help?'

Gamatea silenced her with a lifted hand. She did not take her eyes from the water. At last she subsided on to her haunches and buried her face in her hands. For a while, she rocked to and fro.

'What is to be done? How can we heal this hatred?'

A little white jerboa, like a long-legged mouse, came hopping across the floor to her. It raised its huge, dark eyes and waggled its saucer-like ears. It did not speak aloud, but Gamatea took her hands from her face and looked down at it. Her mouth softened in a smile.

'Yes, Dreamteller, you're right. We must bring them here. I must bring her *here. But this is a task beyond your bravery. The desert is too wide.'*

She got to her feet and walked from the dark pool to the growing light from the door. A shaft of sunlight fell on her

23

curiously patterned cloak. It was intricately embroidered with the dropped feathers of birds, the sloughed skins of snakes, tufts of stray hair from sandy camels, black and white cats, brown rodents.

She gave a sad, wise smile to the doorkeeper, then pursed her lips in a fluting whistle. The blue sky above the flat roofs and palm trees darkened with wings. Hawks and crows, magpies and finches, owls and swallows, birds of every size and colour came flocking down to the steps of the temple.

The Guardian raised her hands in blessing. 'Thank you, all my brothers and sisters. But today I have need of the smallest and most inconspicuous of you. Those who can go even into the midst of our enemies and not raise an eyebrow. I need the help of the sparrows.'

With a chatter of excitement, a crowd of little brown birds hopped forward to her feet. Gamatea knelt before them, her cloak spilling down the steps. She parted them into little flocks. She whispered to each, and they fluttered their wings and cheeped their willingness.

'You to the Mount of Lemon Trees. You to the border. And you to the oasis.'

They rose in a rush of brown wings, wheeled once over the temple's pyramid and took off for the desert.

'And you,' she selected a last plain little bird with a black cap and bib, 'must fly to Mount Femarrat itself. Come with me.'

She cupped the remaining bird in her hands and carried it inside. Crossing the black floor, past the now-quiet pool, she entered a smaller room. The walls were covered with shelves full of rolls of papyrus.

Gamatea sat at her desk and cut a tiny square of paper. She selected the finest-nibbed pen and wrote on it in minute letters. Then she folded it still smaller and sealed it with the merest spot of wax. On the outside she penned a name.

The white jerboa perched on one side of the desk, the sparrow on the other. They watched her with eyes as bright as her own.

'You have a very small leg,' she smiled at the sparrow. 'How shall I manage this?'

From a drawer of her desk she took a roll of narrow gold ribbon. Very carefully, she bound the little letter to the slender bone of the bird's leg. He flapped his wings, adjusting his balance.

'You understand what you have to do? Deliver it to her and no one else. The future of Mount Femarrat and the fate of all our people depend on you.'

The sparrow cheeped. The jerboa looked at the letter with round, thoughtful eyes.

Gamatea carried the bird back to the steps, as if, even now, she was reluctant to let it go. Then, in a swift movement, she cast it from her. The sparrow shot forward across the square. For a moment, the gold ribbon was a flash of sunshine, and then it was too small to see. Up over the rooftops the little bird climbed. It was lost to sight before it reached the edge of the desert.

The Guardian drew a deep breath. She looked down at the jerboa at her feet. 'I am taking a great risk, Dreamteller.'

The day wore on. The horn summoned the Ring-Holders for the sunset ceremony.

'That's us!' Sarba said, as though she could not believe it. 'Have we still got to go through with it? As if this was just a normal day?'

'Now, more than ever, I should have thought. We need the Power.'

Twenty-four Ring-Holders formed a close-knit group. There were guards at the edge of the township. They recognized Letizal's authority as Chief Ring-Holder and passed them through. For the second time that day, Sarba began the long ascent to the summit.

The glare of the bare white rock was fading. She cast her eyes down to the smooth green stone of the staircase at her feet. Veins and whorls of black were trapped within its gleaming surface. As she began to climb, they seemed to ripple like weeds under water.

You're only concentrating on the stairs because you're afraid to think about what's happened, she told herself.

It was true. She saw it in the anxious haste of the other Ring-Holders, stepping on to the staircase, climbing towards the temple. Twenty-four who would form the Evening Circle, working their magic for the Sorcerer Guard in the Control Room. Magic which had been violated.

She was scared. They all were: the Ring-Holders, the sorcerers, everyone. Anger hung like a thundercloud over the sacred mountain. Lightning flashes erupted from the Fence which made a protective girdle around the base of the mountain. Sarba thought of the Control Room, deep in the rock, of the twenty-four sorcerers always on duty. Sorcery was no easy thing. Even now, they would be exerting their combined will to maintain not only the magical Fence she could see below her, but the great border Fence, which stretched across the hills to the west. Her father had often warned them, it meant life or death.

But the Fence had been breached and the culprits had not yet been caught. Something had shaken the mountain itself.

Sarba stole a glance at the faces of the other Ring-Holders, from girls younger than herself with a single band, to Letizal with seven. They were all like her, people in shock. She thought they looked back at her even more fearfully, and knew why. She was Lord Cozuman's daughter. It was her father, above all, who had been mocked.

Kelith shot her a little smile of sympathy. It made Sarba feel marginally better.

She stopped for breath and looked back. Four sorcerers in crimson uniform were climbing behind them. Her heart gave a sudden lift. Wasn't the last of them the tall, free-striding figure of Tekran?

The young sorcerer caught up with her. His hair, the dark gold of ripe wheat, waved on his forehead. She could not see the expression in his eyes.

He did not turn his head to smile at her. They were on duty. His lips barely moved as he murmured, 'They've found Balgo. He claims the others escaped from him in the tunnels. Digonez went after them. That explosion you heard was him smashing the cave where he lost them.'

'What does that mean? Are Alalia and her Xerappans dead... or free?'

He shook his head.

She climbed in front of him. Three more steps to the summit. As she mounted the last, the brief warmth of Tekran's presence vanished. She could no longer shut out the reality of what had happened here this morning, or failed to happen.

What was shocking was that no one had cleared away the evidence of this morning's disaster. Blossoms lay everywhere. Flowers still wreathed the black pillars; flowers strewed the white floor, forming a carpet to the centre; flowers were heaped around the red Stone. All dead now, withered by the day's heat. Or scorched, Sarba could not help thinking, by her father's fury.

The Chief Ring-Holder, Letizal, was outraged. 'Did those idiots at the noon ceremony do nothing about it? Get rid of this mess!' she screamed at them. It was unlike her usual composed, commanding self.

Hastily, Sarba started to untie the garland round the nearest pillar. Kelith was busy on the next one. Younger Ring-Holders were sweeping up armfuls from the floor, while the older ones cleansed the Stone of colourless petals and curled leaves. They stood awkwardly, clutching the damning evidence, and looked to Letizal for guidance. It was a long way back down the stair.

'Throw them over the edge!' The Chief Ring-Holder stamped her foot. The short red cloak around her shoulders flared. Sarba had never seen her so agitated. It made her feel more frightened.

She and Kelith moved beyond the pillared circle of the temple into the last moments of sunshine on the edge of the platform. The sides of the summit were precipitously steep. They cast their arms outwards. The debris of blossoms, still faintly fragrant, drifted down, caught sideways on a little breeze, and scattered in a dusty stain down the pure white slopes. It will be weeks, thought Sarba, before the wind blows them all away, out of our sight. We will not be allowed to forget.

She had not seen her father or Digonez since, and she did not want to. When the Sorcerer Guard caught Alalia Yekhavu, as they surely would, if she was still alive… She turned chill at the thought, as though she were herself the hunted girl.

The Chief Ring-Holder had regained her self-control. She put the long bronze horn to her lips and blew.

There were footsteps on the stairs, the firm tread of booted feet, not the slap of the Ring-Holders' sandals. The four waiting sorcerers rose into view, three men, one woman. Gone were the white dress uniforms of the morning's ceremony. They wore their plain dark red. As the last one mounted the platform, it felt more than usually good to Sarba that it was Tekran on duty this evening.

Then she saw that his mouth, usually so ready to twitch in a smile, was tense. As everyone's was. On Mount Femarrat, in the place where the Children of Yadu should have been most safe, their security had been breached. Any of them might have been killed. Or poisoned, like Sarba's mother.

She must not allow herself to think about that. Nor must she think about what had happened this morning. All that mattered was this hour, now. They must remake the Circle.

The twenty-four Ring-Holders formed a chain inside the pillars. The four sorcerers stepped between them, one taking up position at each point of the compass. Tekran was nearest to her, so that she saw only the back of his fair head. The Ring-Holders joined hands, Kelith's warm, dry fingers on her left, the sweatier grip of a Four-Ring man on her right.

Suddenly, Sarba felt again the strength she had missed. This was what they needed, this was how it happened, the power of the Evening Circle to keep them all safe. The Ring-Holders' power wedded to the spells of the sorcerers, here and in their Control Room. How could it have failed today? They could, they *must*, forge it anew.

She felt the hum rising all around. She never truly knew whether they made it in their throats or whether she heard it only in her mind. She only knew that it throbbed through her whole being. Was it they who made the magic, or did the Power take over *them*?

Across the Stone she saw the view of the land of Yadu below, softening at sunset. White houses glimmering among palm trees, the quiet sea. This precious country. Theirs. The Power had given it to them. Her father said so, and he was the High Sorcerer, who knew everything. No one must be allowed to take it away from them, or threaten their safety.

As the hum rose, so that the pillars seemed to throb with it, Letizal spoke a single word. Sarba gripped her neighbours' hands. This moment always thrilled her with a physical shock, making the breath catch in her throat.

At Letizal's command, the four sorcerers raised their spell-rods and pointed them at the red Stone. A different word was spoken by their four voices in unison, though Sarba could not have repeated what it was. Only the sorcerers understood it clearly.

A flash of light shattered the shadows of the temple and out of the copper bowl on the Stone rose high the twisting pillar of red flame.

Sarba knew that the true Power was not in the Stone or in the flame, yet it was impossible not to feel that it was.

She had renewed the flame: now it was the sorcerers' responsibility to use the power the Ring-Holders gave them.

As the flame steadied and sank, Sarba's breath was not the only one let out in a long sigh. The hum transmuted itself into the hymn of blessing for the night. Still the Circle held, hand within hand, ringing the Stone, ringing the temple, ringing the mountain. We are the Ring-Holders, she thought. We protect this. Not just Mount Femarrat, but the whole land, the Children of Yadu, everything. If we did not make this Circle every day, the enemy would breach our defences and destroy us. She felt proud, powerful, almost motherly, filled with love for everything and everyone around her.

Tekran turned. He caught her eye and colour flooded her face. Of course she loved him. She loved every one of the Children of Yadu. That was her job. The smile he gave her was a little twisted, anxious. The disaster of this morning was far from over. Her lips went on singing. Her eyes tried to reassure him, but part of her was wanting reassurance from him. If the Sorcerer Guard was worried about their safety, they should all be.

The last of the hymn echoed under the ring of the temple roof. The flame burned steadily. It was fiercer than it had been this morning, with the sunlight no longer pouring down on that central Stone. In the morning others would come back to renew it; again at noon they would make another Great Circle. They would never let it die.

She turned towards the steps.

'Sarba.' The Chief Ring-Holder's voice arrested her. 'Hania.' The Six-Ring-Holder halted too.

Sarba's eyes flew to Kelith's face with a look which said, 'Go on. I'll tell you what this is about later.'

Letizal waited until everyone else had left, white robes flowing down the green staircase between white rock, with the dark red flash of the sorcerers' uniforms. When they had gone, it was very quiet. A little breeze whispered between the pillars and the flame on the Stone hissed.

'Sisters, you do not need me to tell you how very serious was what happened here today.' Letizal's lips seemed to move with difficulty. The words came stiff, disjointed.

Sarba felt again that profound fear. She had believed, like everyone else, that her father was all-powerful.

It was hard for the Chief Ring-Holder, too, to admit that he was not. Her words denied the doubt. 'Lord Cozuman has taken control of the situation. He summoned a meeting of the Council an hour ago. Don't be afraid. The traitors may have escaped the mountain, but the High Sorcerer has ensured that he knows exactly where they are. Digonez is leading a detachment of the Sorcerer Guard out to capture them.'

Sarba stifled a tiny gasp. She had seen the fury in her cousin's face here in this temple, when his betrothed failed to appear. What would happen to Alalia when he arrested her?

It was irrational to feel sorry for someone who had run off with two Xerappans.

'It appears that the bride's brother, Balgo Yekhavu, has disappeared again.'

This time Hania and Sarba did gasp in dismay. Balgo was their friend.

The Chief Ring-Holder raised her hand. 'It may not be quite as it seems. If he is with them, then intentionally or not, Balgo will lead Digonez to their escape route. We know there are

31

rebel Xerappans in those hills. This may be our opportunity to crush them, once and for all.

'But clearly, the Yekhavu family are under grave suspicion. We are holding the mother here. She's hysterical after what happened this morning, understandably. I think it's genuine, unless she's a very good actress. Not surprisingly, the betrothal of her daughter to the High Sorcerer's nephew was a union she valued highly.

'Yet it seems surprising that the bride's father didn't come to Mount Femarrat for this ceremony. He's governor of the colony of the Mount of Lemon Trees beyond the border Fence. He gave as his excuse that he had wind of trouble among the local Xerappan population and thought it unwise to leave his post. But there are rumours that he is too friendly with these Xerappans. Lord Cozuman thinks this needs to be investigated.

'The Council is sending an examination team. It will be composed of seven of the Sorcerer Guard and two Ring-Holders. Colonel Gordoz will be in charge. You two will perform the necessary daily ceremonies for the party. Needless to say, beyond the Fence, we need the Power to guard the Children of Yadu even more.'

'But they have sorcerers and Ring-Holders of their own on the Mount of Lemon Trees,' Hania pointed out.

'After what happened this morning, we can trust nobody. If there is treachery among our colleagues there, you must uncover it. Hania, it will be particularly your responsibility to interrogate the colony's Ring-Holders. Sarba will assist you.'

Sarba wanted to cry out, 'Me? But I'm only a Two-Ring-Holder. I'm just fifteen.' She did not. Her training on Mount Femarrat forbade her to question the Chief Ring-Holder.

And besides, was she not Lord Cozuman's only daughter? She knew people expected great things of her because of that. A thrill ran through her. Had her father himself chosen her?

32

Had he singled her out for this, though he had rarely spoken to her since she had left his house as a child?

A little voice cautioned her that the High Sorcerer was not so soft-hearted.

Something else held back her protest. Despite the shock and doubt, part of her was leaping in excitement. She would venture beyond the border Fence, into the Xerappan lands which were being opened up to Yadu colonies. She had never travelled that far. She would be a pioneer, carrying the Power into enemy territory. She was entrusted with an important mission on which the safety of her country depended. She could not wait to tell Kelith.

She sped down the sunset mountain in a daze, in danger of falling down the steep, smooth steps.

Chapter Four

Lord Cozuman summoned them next day, in the hour before noon. A uniformed sorcerer met Hania and Sarba at the foot of the temple staircase as they were descending from making the Noon Circle.

'Report to the High Sorcerer's office immediately,' he ordered both of them, handing them written confirmation from Cozuman's secretary. 'He doesn't like to be kept waiting.' Nothing in his face or speech betrayed that he knew Sarba was the High Sorcerer's daughter.

She did not need to be told that her father demanded absolute, immediate obedience. A queer lump of excitement rose in her throat, part panic, part pride, making it hard to breathe. In all her fifteen years, she had never been to her father's office, from which he ruled the land of Yadu. Even when she had lived in the house, Lord Cozuman had not been a man to mix business with family.

It meant she was now someone of importance, a Ring-Holder worthy of being chosen for a special mission. Just for a moment, she wondered if it was simply favouritism, that she should have been picked out so young. She dismissed the idea instantly. Her father had spent so little time with her, she hardly knew him; but the whole of Yadu knew that he was not a man to allow any softness to influence his judgement. She must, astonishingly, have been chosen on merit... unless Letizal had given flattering reports of her, in the vain hope of earning his favour.

She threw Kelith a flashing smile before she and Hania turned back to the high green staircase. Coming down at the end of their shift, she had felt hot and weary, ready for the midday meal and a rest. Now she felt a rush of energy.

Another flight of steps branched off to the right to Cozuman's house. Not mine now, thought Sarba, though I was born there.

These steps led them to a bare white platform, carved out of the mountainside. Her eyes ached with the intensity of light. A high, blank wall surrounded the house, only relieved by the dark foliage of cypress trees within its compound. Hania spoke the password, and the sorcerer sentries on the gate passed them through.

The courtyard, at least, was familiar. Was it only two days since that eve-of-betrothal party for Digonez and Alalia? Two days since she had first seen the disturbing face of that strange Xerappan boy, with his conquered people's uncanny skill at controlling animals. Seen him whispering to Alalia. She had been right to fear him.

As they walked across the courtyard to the shade of the trees, more distant, bittersweet memories assaulted her. Under these trees, her mother had danced, in and out of the dappled shade, holding out her hands to little Sarba. It seemed impossible now that a man as terrifying as her father could have married a woman who danced and laughed like that. But he had. Sarba was the result of their union.

The dark mouth of the door was open. Another sentry directed them to the long, unadorned corridor down which she had trespassed that evening. Under her feet she began to sense again the throb of the Control Room. Hania turned her head to Sarba with the same gleam of comprehension. They both heard it now, felt it. The floor shook beneath their feet and faintly they caught the swell of chanting from many throats. Here was the sorcery which defended them against the Xerappans.

The door at the end of the corridor was ajar. They could hear voices. Hania tapped on it.

Her father's secretary opened it. His red-and-white robe swung from the speed with which he had crossed the room. The others standing inside wore the red tunic and trousers of the Sorcerer Guard.

Lord Cozuman was seated at his desk, with his back to the window. It was hard to see his shaded face clearly. Today, his loose red robe was faced with white and black. The walls of his room were white, banded with red and black. Red and black borders outlined the open windows. For a strange moment, she saw him as part of this house, part of Mount Femarrat, as painted stone.

Then he turned his face to her, and she knew he was more intensely alive than anyone else in that room. His face was as craggy as an eagle's. He looked older than she knew he was. The piercing grey-blue eyes held hers, as though he saw right through to her soul. He registered her presence, but said nothing. His gaze turned to Hania. Still silence.

The light from the window caught the plain gold circle on his grey hair: the crown of the High Sorcerer. Rumour said that when Cozuman put it on, he could see into the thoughts of anyone, anywhere in the land of Yadu. In his presence, it was possible to believe that.

His eyes counted the Ring-Holders and sorcerers standing in front of him. 'Seven. It wants two yet.' There was the slightest edge of menace in his voice. What would happen if someone came late?

Now, as the tension of arrival was retreating, she could look properly at the others. Colonel Gordoz she had expected: stocky, rather short for a Yadu, but with an evident air of energy. His lieutenant, Undiliz, followed him like a shadow, always imitating his colonel, even trying to outdo him to show his loyalty. And a tall, younger sorcerer, turning his head...

Shock, joy! Tekran had been chosen too. She saw the answering light of pleasure in his eyes. This she had not expected, would not even have allowed herself to dream of. She and Tekran, on the same mission.

So it was a few seconds more before she registered the two remaining sorcerers. One was a woman, wearing the same red tunic and trousers as the men. Her face was plain, square-jawed, with a defiant tilt to it, as though to assert that she, as much as any of them, could uphold the fearsome reputation of the Sorcerer Guard.

Did Tekran feel like that? It was hard to imagine his face scaring people. But all the Sorcerer Guard had a job to do. They could not afford to be soft. She would not want them to be.

There was one more behind the others. A chill crawled over Sarba's skin. Always Vendel seemed to be standing in shadow. It was as if he carried shadow with him. Tall, silent. His face might have been carved out of some ancient tree root. Yet, unlike her father's, it did not blaze into that sudden active intensity. Vendel's intensity lay in his stillness. His was a mind too deep for anyone to read, unless it were Cozuman. Sarba realized she feared to make this journey with Vendel as much as she rejoiced at making it with Tekran.

She wrenched her eyes away. She needed to look at something pleasanter. Tekran, on duty, had prudently turned his attention back to Lord Cozuman.

Beyond her father's shoulders, the window openings showed her no view of the courtyard and its gardens. This room must lie at the very brink of the precipitous mountain slope. An intelligent part of her mind saw the wisdom. Nothing said in this room could be heard by anyone outside. It looked straight out on a stunning view of Yadu's coast. Palms and fig trees made a luxury of green to rest the eyes. The beach was pure silver, brilliant with the foam of breakers.

The sea was an achingly dark purple-blue. It was impossible to look on this land and not love it.

As if guided by an intelligence not her own, Sarba's eyes came back to her father's desk. It was bare, save for a single folder with a leather cover, which must contain the details of their mission – and one small painting in an ebony frame. It was angled, so that she could glimpse what it was. Her mother's face. The young, laughing mother of her childhood, not the twisted, drooling face it had become.

She lifted her eyes to the window again. To the far left of the beach she could just see the fishing village where her mother was being nursed through her mindless days. Every week Sarba went to visit her. On the terrace above that beach, under those pines, she would hold her mother's hand, talk and sing to her, never expecting any response.

Her gaze went back to that little portrait, the only spark of humanity in this stark, disciplined office. Here her father would work out his own revenge.

There was a brisk rap on the door. The secretary let in the last two sorcerers. They were not men Sarba knew.

'Examiner Orzad, my lord, and Sergeant Ilian.'

Sarba gave a start of curiosity. She did not think she had met an Examiner before. She noticed at once that he was wearing loose robes, not the tunic and trousers of most of the Guard, whose differently coloured epaulettes announced their rank. The military wing of the Sorcerer Guard were very evident on Mount Femarrat, carrying out duties to enforce its security. They were by far the majority of the sorcerers. They took their turns at holding fast the spells in the Control Room; they supplied four sorcerers to take the Power from the flame at the Circle ritual; they guarded the mountain. But there were others who worked more secretly, finding the intelligence without which no spell-rods could keep them safe. Orzad must be one of those. Of course. Intelligence about the

38

Yekhavu family was what this was all about.

She looked at him now with increased awe. It was not a remarkable face, rather broad and pleasant. It did not chill her like the silent Vendel's. You felt you could trust a man like this, talk to him. How many had talked to Orzad, to their own downfall?

She did not dwell on the man behind him, apologetically squeezing into the room, as though there was less space than there really was. He was a plump sorcerer, whose face would have been cheerful under any other circumstances. He did not look particularly alarming, or, for that matter, of any great intelligence.

A second later, it occurred to her that there must be more to him. It was not her father's nature to have chosen these nine lightly. But she had no time to look back at the sergeant. Lord Cozuman was speaking.

That sharp, cold voice spoke directly in her heart. It did not seem as though the sound reached her through her ears. He seemed to be speaking to her alone. So, she was sure, it felt to everyone else. His words held her, demanded her whole attention, her absolute obedience. She did not know if he put a spell upon his hearers, but it felt like that.

She listened with a kind of terror, afraid she might miss something of crucial importance and fail him.

'Sorcerers and Ring-Holders, you have been chosen to be the eyes and ears of Yadu. It is a grave responsibility. I know you will not fail me.' An unexpected, brilliant smile, as when the sun breaks through black storm clouds. This was what she remembered from those too-brief times with him in her childhood. He would arrive in their living quarters, stiff and stern from the day's responsibilities. Her mother would hand him a beaker of cool pomegranate juice, run her hand lightly through his hair, as if he were not the feared High Sorcerer, pick up Sarba and tell Cozuman the clever or foolish things she had done that day. It took time to soften him. He answered briefly, preoccupied at first. Then, her mother's gaiety and love would break through to him, and she and Sarba would be treated to that rare, radiant smile. She had lived for those moments. Since her mother's illness, they had been denied her.

But he would still use the power of that smile, knowing its hold over people, to pursue his policies and bind his officers to him. Men and women would go beyond the call of duty for that smile.

A murmur of assent, of unqualified loyalty met him. Sarba's voice was there with all the rest.

'To be the governor of a colony beyond the Fence is a high privilege. Such people hold the future of Yadu in their hands. Soon, all that was once the land of the Xerappans, who hate us, will be ours.' Another burst of enthusiasm. 'In the hands of the colonies' governors are our destiny, our glory and our safety.

'Jentiz Yekhavu is such a man. Governor of the Mount of Lemon Trees colony. That his daughter – *his daughter!* – should break her promise to my nephew and escape from Mount Femarrat with her Xerappan chariot driver and maid is one of the most shocking acts of treachery in our history. It is not only Digonez she mocks, but Mount Femarrat and the Sorcerer Guard, the temple and its Ring-Holders. The sanctity of the land of Yadu itself.'

His voice in her heart spoke more grief than anger. She, a Child of Yadu, shared his pain.

The voice became steely. 'Treachery. Three things are imperative. That we catch Alalia Yekhavu and punish her, thoroughly and publicly. That we find what lured her to such a shameful act of rebellion, and see that it can never happen again. That we discover who were her accomplices, who knew or suspected what was in her mind and failed to report it.

Above all, who influenced her. The greatest suspicion must fall on the family who raised her.

'Since last night, Digonez has been tracking them. I have just had his report. He has caught up with them. Her brother Balgo is dead.'

Sarba could not repress her gasp of pity and horror. She heard the same from Tekran. Balgo Yekhavu, the boy they had laughed and sung with in the tavern on summer evenings, dead?

'He resisted arrest.' Cozuman's voice dismissed pity. 'Their mother is still here, being questioned. An hysterical woman, I fear.

'There remains, more interestingly, the father, Jentiz Yekhavu. He chose not to attend the ceremony. It may have been, as he said, concern about rumours of some disaffection among the Xerappans living near his colony. In the light of what happened, it may not have been. It may indicate a less than complete desire to see his daughter betrothed to my nephew.' The menace in his voice had become icy. 'Daughters do not arrive at their view of life single-handed. Parents have a crucial influence. What was there in her background to persuade Alalia Yekhavu she would rather run away with a degenerate leopard handler than become the wife of the officer who may well be the next High Sorcerer?'

Digonez. Her handsome, supremely confident cousin. The son her father must have wished for, and never had. Sarba knew there was an assumption among her friends that she would one day be the Chief Ring-Holder. Had she been wrong to protest that Cozuman would show no favouritism? For all his apparent neglect of her, family was, it seemed, important to Cozuman.

'Orzad,' he turned to the robed Examiner, 'the interrogation of Jentiz Yekhavu is a task for you.' The Examiner nodded. 'You may find it helpful to make Jentiz aware that we still hold his wife. Tekran will act as your assistant.'

A fist constricted Sarba's heart. It was hard to think of the gentle Tekran in the context of this threat of... what?... torture? What was happening to Alalia's mother?

'Hania, there are two Ring-Holders on the Mount of Lemon Trees. They share the burden with others in neighbouring colonies. You must find out how loyal they are. There is, I regret to observe, an occasional tendency for colonists to go, as they say, *native*. You will discover if there is any inappropriate siding with the Xerappans. Never forget, we are still at war. The battles in which the sorcerers triumphed over them were swift, but we would be foolish to relax our vigilance until their last resistance is crushed.

'Vendel, you and Innerta will make the same enquiries among the colony's sorcerers.' Sarba's instinctive recoil from the name of that tall, silent shadow delayed for a moment her understanding of the second name. Innerta must be the pugnacious-looking female sorcerer, whom Sarba had never met before. They looked an oddly matched pair.

'What about the Xerappans, sir?' Colonel Gordoz could not keep the eagerness out of his voice.

Cozuman looked almost amused. 'Yes, Colonel, that is a job I think you and Lieutenant Undiliz would handle particularly well. The local sorcerers have, of course... *visited*... the boy's family.' There was a throaty chuckle from the colonel and his lieutenant. 'His younger sister, I regret to say, was Alalia's maid, and part of their plot to escape from Mount Femarrat. When caught, as she will be, she will be treated as a dangerous enemy to the state. Unfortunately, their parents had fled. There were only two grandparents left. Their farmhouse has, naturally, been destroyed, but I wonder if the methods used on the old people were quite as persuasive as they could have been.'

'You can trust us to put that right, sir.'

'I'm sure I can. Which leaves the rest of the colonists, who are not sorcerers or Ring-Holders. You must share their interrogation among yourselves. Colonel Gordoz, you will organize this.'

Gordoz, and not the more intelligent-looking Examiner Orzad? Yet from the ready way the colonel nodded his assent and looked his team over, she saw his organizing ability, his assumption of leadership. The Examiner, marked out from the others by his robes, looked more like a man who would operate on his own. She saw a glance of understanding pass between him and the High Sorcerer. A cold suspicion crept over her. Was there another reason for Orzad to be here on this team? Not only for his investigative skill and experience, but to report on his fellow team-members?

The next words caught her unawares. 'Of particular interest, of course, will be Alalia's closest friends. I find it incredible that they will not know something. Girls gossip. Explicitly or implicitly, Alalia Yekhavu is sure to have confided something to them of her thoughts about her betrothal, of her relations with Xerappans, of her commitment, or otherwise, to the land of Yadu. You, Sarba, will discover this.'

The shock was like a wave of cold water in her face. A heartbeat later, she realized she should have expected this. Nothing her father did was accidental. If he had chosen her for this mission, at fifteen, it must have been for a reason more significant than that she was a promising servant of the Power of the Ring, and his daughter.

She was a similar age to Alalia and her friends, Yadu girls like herself. They would easily trust her, talk to her. Without Hania or the sorcerers present, they would forget she was as much an investigator as the other eight. She would, she must, must win their confidence… and betray it.

Cozuman rose from his desk. He walked across to the wall

and pointed his spell-rod at a map of the Yadu and Xerappan lands. Sarba was jolted back into the present. Had that map been there all the time? She could not remember it, only a wall of plain white, red and black plaster.

This map was alive with other colours. Blue sea shimmered along its eastern edge. The coastal plain was the rich green of farmland and orchards, flickering with the movement of people. There was the white cone of Mount Femarrat, with its black temple on the summit, its base ringed by the silvery Fence. This mountain was the centre of the whole map, the most dazzling, vibrant thing. The headquarters of the Sorcerer Guard and the Ring-Holders. She knew a surge of pride.

Cozuman's rod moved further west. Beyond the lush farms rose golden hills. Vegetation petered out on their dusty slopes. Between their ridges were deeply shadowed clefts, impenetrably black. Though it was still within Yadu, this was alien territory, where she had never been. Even on the map, the border Fence along the crest of those hills looked massive, pulsing with powerful spells. Surely, the lethal magic in that could keep anything out? But treachery had struck, more than once, inside their borders.

Still the spell-rod moved on. Beyond the Fence, the map became mistier, the colours softer, the detail harder to define. This must be Xerappo, or all that was left of it. Once, it had been a great kingdom stretching down to the sea. But the Children of Yadu had claimed it for themselves since the war. Rightly, Lord Cozuman told them, by their descent from one of its queens. In any case, what claim could a people without magic, like the Xerappans, have on sacred Mount Femarrat?

There were little spots of light pulsing in this sand-coloured wilderness. Tiny Fences, ringing the colonies. Small patches of green marked their plantations. A more faded grey-green, without Fences, stained the valleys. Xerappan villages?

Cozuman's spell-rod moved in and touched the wall-map.

As that square of the grid suddenly magnified, everyone started, except the suave secretary.

'The Mount of Lemon Trees. Governed by Jentiz Yekhavu.'

The enlargement had not produced as much clarity as Sarba would have liked. It was grainy, its spots of colour spread more thinly over the parchment. Yet she could pick out individual houses, roads, even trees, though as indistinct smudges of white, or yellow, or green. Excitement rose in her throat, nearly choking her. She was going there. She could almost believe she saw people, small as dust motes, moving about the township.

The realization caught up with her with renewed force. Those were real people, though she could not yet make out their faces. Some of them would be girls like herself, Alalia's friends. These were the people she would be investigating covertly. She must find out their secrets and reveal them to Cozuman, whatever the consequences. This was her mission for her country.

'Sergeant Ilian, as you know, this region is unsuitable for horses. You'll be in charge of the camels, and the expedition's supplies.'

'Understood, my lord!' They all turned. The plump sergeant had remained squeezed into the space by the door, almost apologetically. Now he swelled with pride and eagerness. So this was what he had been summoned for. His words tumbled over each other. 'Never you fear, sir. Camels may have a bad reputation in the barracks as surly beasts, but there's nothing you can't do with them, once you win their confidence. I knew one once...'

'Thank you, Sergeant.' Her father almost smiled. 'I think we can take it the mounts will be in safe hands.'

He turned back to the map. His rod moved sideways from the Mount of Lemon Trees. Past its green fields, with their orderly rows of fruit trees and vegetables, to one of those

45

grey-green smudges beside a tiny stream. It came to rest on what looked like a tumble of stones, hardly distinguishable in colour from the dusty soil.

'The Xerappan farm, where Alalia Yekhavu's chariot driver and maid lived, whom we allowed inside our Fence, on to sacred Mount Femarrat.' Cozuman's voice had sunk to a furious hiss. 'The house is no more, but the grandparents are still squatting in the ruins. Gordoz.' He turned a smile on the colonel more chilling than a scowl could ever have been. 'You will know how to make them talk.'

Chapter Five

She would not be sleeping that afternoon.

'Madam.' She bowed to the Chief Ring-Holder. 'We're leaving Mount Femarrat tomorrow. I don't know when we'll be back. Is it possible...? I know it's four days to my next day off, when I usually visit my mother, but I'm not sure when I'll be able to see her again.'

She waited nervously, hardly daring to lift her eyes. A Ring-Holder was supposed to abandon all claims to family, to serve only the Power and the land of Yadu. She had made a preliminary vow when she entered the order at fourteen. Only last week, she had confirmed it when she was given her second ring. She might visit that little village of Shells on the coast on her one free day, but it must never interfere with her work.

Letizal's silence made it impossible not to look up. The Chief Ring-Holder's face was stern, her lips compressed. Instinct, Sarba knew, was making her want to refuse outright and scold Sarba roundly for even asking.

The older woman gave the smallest of sighs. 'Your preparations for the journey can hardly be lengthy, I suppose. A Ring-Holder needs few possessions. You'll need writing materials, a few clothes. Hania will tell you what to take for the ceremonies. I've discussed that with her. So, yes, I suppose you would be back for the Evening Circle.'

'Easily! Three hours is all I need.'

Letizal nodded, as though a spoken agreement would have

made her complicit in some sense of wrongness. She turned away.

'Thank you, madam!'

Sarba fled.

As she raced back to her hostel, she wondered again how much the fact that she was Lord Cozuman's daughter had counted. It should not have done. Rules were rules. Vows were sacred.

There was no time to think. She looked around the hostel compound quickly. Normally, she set out in the cool of the morning, passed through Mount Femarrat's Fence, then strolled out towards the coast and its long beach. She picked wild flowers on the way, whatever was in season. Silly, she knew. The gardens of the clinic were expensively beautiful. But it was the only gift she had found which seemed to have any meaning for her mother. Sometimes she thought she saw a glimmer of pleasure in those eyes.

Today, there would be no time to walk through the fields.

There was a jacaranda tree in the courtyard, spreading its shade and dropping a carpet of lilac-coloured petals. Sarba checked that no one was watching, reached up and broke off four sprays of blossom. It was enough for an armful. She buried her nose in it. The wood was as fragrant as the flowers.

She crossed to the sorcerer at the gate. 'Would you call me a chariot, please?'

'For one?'

'Yes.'

He did not draw his spell-rod for so trivial a thing. Instead, he mounted the stair to the roof of the guard post. A mirror flashed in the sun.

Sarba shivered in the noonday heat. Sorcery was a more serious business than that. Those white-and-gold spell-rods the sorcerers wore were there only to keep this country secure. And it was Ring-Holders like her whose Circle called

48

down the Power on which that sorcery depended.

The sorcerer shouted down to her, 'It'll be at the main exit by the time you get there.'

'Thank you.'

She walked down to the perimeter gate, or rather, to the place where the gate would appear. The road led down to the foot of the mountain, and on beyond. The Fence stretched, unbroken, across it. There were many sentries on duty today, an air of palpable tension. More sorcerers patrolled the perimeter.

Sarba tried not to look at the Fence. Yet it was difficult not to, and when she did, it made her feel strange, almost sick.

At the first glance, it seemed just a barrier, three times her height, made of a silvery diamond-patterned mesh. But look at it only for a second, and it came to disturbing life. Shimmering serpents slithered up and down its strands, zigzagging, criss-crossing, looming ever larger as she looked, thrusting their heads towards her, their glittering eyes growing wider, till she was first giddy and then terrified.

It never got any better. It was not meant to. Mount Femarrat was well guarded.

Or it had been, until yesterday.

'Show your identification!' The sharpness in the sentry's voice told her this was not the first time he had asked her.

She wanted to say, 'Don't be silly, Rolan. You know who I am.' She did not. When a sorcerer took up duty at the entry to the sacred mountain, all personal friendships were left behind. Sarba was as much an object of suspicion as a perfect stranger.

Obediently, she held up her wrist, with its carnelian bracelet. She felt his spell-rod play over it, a tingling sensation. She was aware of being watched keenly by an older man on the other side of the path.

'This side too, please,' the other sentry said, when Rolan had passed her as harmless.

This was unusual. Checks were thorough for those coming in, but the staff of Mount Femarrat were hardly suspects when they were on their way out.

The second sorcerer was satisfied. What came next was even more disturbing. But it always was. Together the sorcerers spoke the spell of opening. This time she heard the words, but no keenness of hearing, no effort of memory, could ever recall them. She did not know what language they were spoken in and never would. It was not just a tongue she hadn't learned, but one she never could learn. Only a sorcerer could. Anyone else could not even remember the words, let alone understand them. Not even a Ring-Holder.

The serpents writhed. The whole Fence began to move. Panels of it were folding in zigzags, doubling against each other, so that the snakes clustered ever more thickly, their silver scales brilliant. The barrier was withdrawing on either side of the road.

Even now, she was aware that something was different. There must be at least eight sorcerers massed behind her, blocking the way in. Why? There was no one outside, only the chariot she had ordered, waiting a prudent way off.

What were they afraid of? Could a runaway Yadu girl and two Xerappan servants have made such a difference? Was Mount Femarrat really in danger? There had been a whisper of poison found in the courtyard. She blocked that thought out.

She steeled her nerves to walk between the folded pillars of the Fence. The charge of magic thrilled through her. It was unpleasant, nothing like the joy she experienced from the Power in the temple.

She heard the words of closing as soon as she stepped outside. She felt very exposed as she walked on down the road, with the Sorcerer Guard still watching her.

It was a one-donkey chariot, on a light wood-and-wicker frame. The donkey was the first thing that made Sarba smile since she had set out. It was pure white, with the sweetest face. The next thing she noticed brought her back with a jolt. The driver was a Xerappan.

Of course, there was nothing unusual about that. Most chariot drivers were. Xerappans had a way with animals, better than most of the Children of Yadu. And those who had stayed in the coastal plain after the war, instead of running away over the hills, had no choice but to work as servants, or in other lowly jobs. It was, after all, what they were fit for. But Sarba could never suppress the instinct to shudder when she saw them. They had done her too much damage.

Today, more than ever, any Xerappan seemed like a threat. The Sorcerer Guard had trusted or ignored Alalia's servants. They had been allowed into Mount Femarrat, as if they were no more than the Yekhavus' baggage. They had proved to be far more than that. She had seen the leopard-driver and Alalia, their heads close together.

She studied this one, under his wide straw hat. His face was darker than hers, and the brim of the hat cast it into deeper shadow. His head was bowed, his eyes downcast. He must have heard her coming, even in her quiet sandals, but he gave no sign.

The donkey twitched its ears.

'Take me to Shells, to the Oleander Clinic.'

'Yes, ma'am.'

He got down from the driving seat to help her up. He was shorter than she was. His baggy trousers were wearing thin at the knees. Long ago, the hems had been embroidered, evidence of hours of intricate work. Now, the once-colourful stitches were faded by the sun and threads were hanging loose. Even the man's clothing looked defeated.

She rejected his helping hand, but she had to sit beside him. The two-wheeled chariot was not big enough for a rear seat. She fought down her revulsion. She had never sat so close to a Xerappan. If only there had been time to walk to Shells as she usually did, alone.

The man called encouragement to his donkey and then lapsed into silence as the chariot began to roll.

The countryside drowsed past in the afternoon heat. People sat in the shade of farmhouses, shelling beans, weaving palm mats. Out in the fields, gangs of Xerappans worked on, under a Yadu master.

It all looked so normal. Was it only Mount Femarrat which was under this cloud of fear?

The bright line of the sea made her eyes ache. She had never acquired the habit of wearing smoked glasses as many sorcerers had. It made them look more threatening when you couldn't see their eyes. The beach was brilliant white. She could smell the seaweed mixed with the fragrance of the jacaranda in her arms. The Xerappan fishing village was coming into view, but she did not need to go quite that far. She could already see the clinic, set amid the restful luxuriance of trees.

'Stop here.' She jumped down before he could come round to help her.

Shells crunched under her feet. It was an incredible beach, as though thousands of people had had a feast of every kind of seafood imaginable and dropped all the shells. Fan-shaped cockles, spiralling conches, fragments of abalone lined with mother-of-pearl. If you looked closely, you could pick out pinks, purples, greens, but the whole mass had been smashed by waves, ground together, trodden by feet, until it was crushed into a carpet that was mostly a glittering white.

It was like climbing the temple staircase this morning: she was concentrating on what was under her feet, so that she would not have to think about what lay ahead.

She was almost there. The feathery shadows of tamarisk trees softened the glare of the beach. She raised her eyes. A lone guard patrolled the beach in front of the clinic. Knowing her as a regular visitor, he checked her Ring-Holder's bracelet only as a formality before waving her past.

There had been more than one guard on the beach that terrible day, but it had not saved the victims from the Xerappans. Should she be angry that this man was so casual? Years of peace had lulled the Yadu into a sense of security, until yesterday. Surely they must have heard what had happened on Mount Femarrat?

Grass underfoot now. There were figures sitting in cushioned chairs on the shaded terrace in front of the house. She could not yet pick out her mother, but she was probably there.

The lawn had been well watered. It was lushly green, recently cut. She could see Xerappan gardeners watering flower-beds further away. A Yadu nurse in a crisp white tunic moved forward between the lolling patients to greet her.

'Miss Cozuman! We weren't expecting you today.'

'I know, but I'm going away tomorrow. I don't know when I'll be able to come again.'

'It's good of you to make the effort, but I've told you before. She can't tell one day from another. She wouldn't know if you missed a visit or not.'

'I expect you're right.' Sarba made the effort to smile. 'I'm probably doing it for me, as much as for her.'

It was not quite true. She clung on to the belief that there might be some spark of consciousness left in her mother, unable to express itself. She had to believe that these visits mattered.

The nurse brought a stool and put it beside her mother's chair. Quessa Cozuman lay on the orange-and-white-striped cushions, her head lolling to one side. Her fair hair, prematurely greying, had been plaited and coiled behind her head for coolness. It left her face cruelly exposed. One corner of her mouth was slackly open, drooling. The lid drooped over her left eye. Sarba bent over and kissed her.

'I've brought you flowers. Jacaranda. They smell lovely.'

She held the flowers to her mother's face. Was that a gleam of recognition in her right eye? Or just a reflection of the sunlight?

She sat down and took her mother's hand. It was wrinkled like an old woman's, the fingers bent together, angling stiffly. Sarba massaged them as she talked. She told her mother all the news. The marvellous party her father had given before the betrothal of Digonez and Alalia. How she and the other Ring-Holders had waited in the temple next morning. The growing alarm when the bride had failed to appear. The shock when the alarm had sounded, telling that someone had tried to breach the perimeter Fence. Digonez's fury, the Sorcerer Guard setting out in pursuit.

She did not, could not, describe to her mother the expression on her father's face. The High Sorcerer's will was absolute, throughout Yadu and even beyond. The unthinkable had happened. A teenage Yadu girl and two young Xerappans had flouted that will.

'I've been chosen for a special mission, to investigate Alalia Yekhavu's family, and the people she knew. It's the first time I've been outside Yadu. I'm going across the border into Xerappo.' She tried to put excitement, pride, confidence into her voice. She wanted her mother to be proud of her, in the very faint hope that she could understand.

She watched that twisted face intently. Her fingers paused in massaging the withered hand. Was there any response? Any pressure against her palm? Any movement of the deformed lips? Any flicker of that eye?

The stillness lengthened. Rage welled up in Sarba, fuelled by self-pity. Wasn't it enough that her father was the High Sorcerer, whose high calling had cut him out of most of her childhood? It was too cruel to take away her mother as well.

It was perhaps the cruellest thing that she had been just old enough to remember the woman Quessa Cozuman had been, but not old enough to retain more than a handful of memories. She played them over again and again. The two of them trying to catch a blue-and-green lizard in the courtyard, laughing as it shot out from under her mother's hands. A dance her mother had performed for her father, with a gauzy red veil floating around her. Sarba lying in her little bed, cradled safe on soft pillows, with her mother crooning a lullaby over her.

Sarba started to sing:

> *'The Power of the stars to guide you,*
> *The Power of the Stone to hold you,*
> *The Power of my love to cradle you,*
> *Sing in the stories I've told you.'*

Her voice threatened to break. With her free hand, she brushed her misted eyes. Would it have been better if her mother had died, like all those others?

Astonishingly, she could not remember that picnic. She only knew what others had told her, much later.

It had been her mother's idea. A beach picnic with her friends and their children at the village of Sea Pines, further up the coast. The war had been won, the Xerappans soundly defeated, but Quessa was the High Sorcerer's wife, so they took along a few of the Sorcerer Guard, just to be sure. The kitchens of their house on Mount Femarrat had provided a hamper of food. It was not that which had killed them.

Other picnickers had been alerted by their screams. By the time they reached the party, it was too late. Most were already beyond the reach of magic. Only a few wailing children remained. None of them was old enough to tell how it happened.

The Sorcerer Guard who investigated the disaster found traces of poison in a gourd which had held the favourite local drink, coconut milk flavoured with honey and rose petals. The kitchen staff swore it had not been in the hamper. Most likely, it had been bought from a Xerappan vendor touting it along the beach. The Yadu picnickers must have passed it round between them. Even the sorcerers guarding them had drunk a share. Grommalan was a deadly poison. The smallest trace could kill. Somehow, her mother and one of the guards had survived, both damaged beyond hope of recovery.

Sarba and four other children were the only ones left unharmed. They were among the youngest. Probably, they had turned up their noses at this unfamiliar drink. Now, even the smell of coconut made Sarba retch.

The Sorcerer Guard's spell-rods had tracked the poisoned gourd back to Sea Pines. They traced its passage through many hands, in half a dozen houses. Everyone associated with it was suspect. The High Sorcerer ordered retribution calculated to make sure that no Xerappan would ever use poison against the Yadu again. That was, of course, just and necessary.

There was an ugly rumour that every man, woman and child in Sea Pines had been massacred. Sarba did not believe that could be true. The authorities on Mount Femarrat had denied it.

Yet looking down at the ruin of her carefree mother, she felt the rage well up in her again. Who were these barbarians who could wreck the lives of her mother, of her father, of Sarba herself, for their political ends? What if they believed, stupidly, they had more right to this land than the Yadu had? Could anything excuse this?

Was it really true, as Tekran had whispered to her, that the sorcerers had found traces of poison in Lord Cozuman's courtyard after the betrothal party, though no one had died? The Xerappan maid, the Xerappan leopard-driver, these were clearly dangerous people. There could be no room for pity.

56

A grim determination was growing within her. She was her father's child. She would go into Xerappo on his mission. She would do whatever he asked. She would find the truth of this treachery and root it out. Never again must the innocent Yadu fall victim like this.

'*The Power of the stars…*', she sang to her mother, holding her hand tighter.

Quessa Cozuman's head turned slightly at the song. Her one good eye seemed to hold Sarba's. The partially paralysed lips quivered.

She mumbled, '*Salamander.*'

A shock ran through Sarba, like the charge of magic she felt when she passed through the Fence.

'What! What did you say?' She bent over her mother eagerly.

The greying head fell back on the pillows. The eyes were vacant. There was no further word.

Salamander. Friends of her mother had told her this was Quessa's pet name for her husband. The idea seemed unthinkable to everyone now. No one on Mount Femarrat ever spoke Lord Cozuman's first name, Saliman.

Yet once, the High Sorcerer had been a young man in love.

Sarba looked round her room to check if there was anything else she needed to pack. The goatskin travel bag was still half empty. What, after all, did she need? Letizal had advised her to take warm clothes. Nights could be cold in the hill country, even in summer. She had her cloak and her winter robe. But the contents of her clothes chest were as simple as this hostel room. She had taken the Ring-Holders' vow never to marry. What did she need with pretty dresses and jewellery? Her white-and-red gown, the carnelian bracelet were all she required. She wore them proudly.

There was still time before the Evening Circle. She moved to the opening in the wall which served as a window and sat down on the chest in front of it. The heat had gone from the sun. Its level rays threw a pathway of gold across the sea, glimpsed between fronds of palm. The hostel itself was already in shadow. Mount Femarrat cast a dark cone of shade across the plain, as the sun sank behind it. The breeze was still warm.

Her arm, with its yellow-red bracelet, lay along the sill. She watched the shifting colours in it as she moved it slightly. It seemed a slender, fragile thing to hold the Power.

A flutter of wings startled her. A sparrow settled on the outside ledge. It was the commonest of birds, an unremarkable colour. Brown back feathers, a whitish underside, with a coal-black bib. Yet, as it hopped closer to her, a flash of gold showed on one twig-like leg. Sarba stared. Her hand reached out instinctively towards it.

She checked it in mid-air. But the sparrow made no move to fly away. Its bright, dark eye stared back at her.

Sarba was trying to make sense of what she was seeing. A band of ribbon had been wrapped round the bird's right leg. It was securing a tiny rectangle of yellow paper.

Still the sparrow waited, its head cocked to one side. More cautiously this time, Sarba advanced her hand. Her fingers brushed soft feathers and then the thin, hard line of the bird's leg. It made no move to fly off, though she could feel the beating of its heart under the breast feathers.

The gold ribbon was sealed with a dab of wax. Carefully, she broke it with her thumbnail and unwound the wrapping. It fell in a softly coloured coil on the window ledge. The yellow paper fell with it. She picked it up. Two edges had been folded together. They too were sealed with a spot of wax. She turned it over. On the other side were written two minute words. She peered closely.

Jentiz Yekbavu.

The shock was almost as great as when her mother had spoken.

Jentiz Yekhavu. A name unknown to her until today. The father of the runaway bride. The governor of the colony on the Mount of Lemon Trees. The man their mission was going to investigate.

She stared at the tiny letter in her hand. It was not for her. So why had the sparrow brought it to her window? It could not possibly be expecting her to deliver it to Jentiz Yekhavu.

But how could the sparrow know? Only a handful of people had been told where she was going. Surely, no one on Mount Femarrat would have given her such a message to deliver. She was the youngest member of the expedition. Yet how could anyone outside have heard about it?

The sparrow, its mission completed, was spreading its wings. Sarba lunged towards it, grabbed at the fluttering bird. It was hasty, ill-judged. There was a pounding of feathers against her palms. The bird broke free, but not quite: a falling strand of Sarba's hair had tangled in its claw. There was a tiny wrench of pain in her scalp. Then the bird was free, and soaring into the evening sky, with a single gold hair from Sarba trailing behind it.

She subsided on to the chest, panting. It had been rash, brutal even. She might have damaged the little bird beyond flying. But there were too many questions fluttering in her head, refusing to be pinned down.

Her heart was pounding like the sparrow's. What did it mean? Was it magic? Surely the bird couldn't have lighted on her window ledge by chance. It had let her take the message from its leg. It *knew*.

But the letter was not for her. *Jentiz Yekhavu*. The name loomed up from the paper, seeming ten times larger than it really was. Who had sent it? Why?

She turned it over again with a shaking hand. The tiny red seal faced her. She could slit it as easily as she had broken the wax on the ribbon. Her thumb tested it.

And fell away.

She was being squeamish. She was a Ring-Holder, charged with keeping Yadu safe. She must either find out what this letter said or take it to Letizal. That was her clear duty.

What would she say to the Chief Ring-Holder? *A sparrow brought it to me?* She could see the cold scorn in Letizal's face. She would never believe that. Sarba could hardly believe it herself. Yet where would she think it had come from?

Fear crawled through her. Letizal's voice spoke in her head: *Sarba Cozuman, have you been in touch with subversives?*

What if they took her to her father, to be interrogated as a traitor? The idea terrified her.

The memory of the bird's bright eye returned to her. She had felt its fear as it let her untie the letter. But it had stayed still until she had finished. It had trusted her. *Why?*

A dangerous temptation was growing in her. Because it knew I wouldn't open it, that I wouldn't betray it?

But I'm the High Sorcerer's daughter.

Only a few hours ago, she had sat by her mother's couch and vowed she would do anything, *anything*, demanded of her to ensure that that horror never happened again. What might happen if she said nothing?

If she broke the seal and read the letter, she could find out how dangerous it was.

And then?

The horn sounded for the Evening Circle. The shadow of Mount Femarrat had almost reached the coast. Sarba stood up, still irresolute.

She dropped the tiny paper into the neck of her robe and left the room.

Chapter Six

The square at the base of Mount Femarrat was filled with off-duty sorcerers and Ring-Holders, gathering in an expectant hush. Sarba joined them, feeling the welcome cooling of the evening shadows. Her eyes found Kelith, and the two girls moved towards each other. Only the Ring-Holders whose watch this was would climb to the temple for the Evening Circle. Everyone else would make it where they could. All across Yadu, activity would cease. Families would link hands. The sorcerers forging spells in the Control Room would pause for a few moments to make a Circle. The sentries on the Fence would draw closer together.

The horn sounded again, from high on the summit. Kelith's hand was in Sarba's, as it had been this morning. On the other side, a man's hand closed round hers. Her blood leaped. She knew, even before she turned, it was Tekran. She did not smile at him, yet. This moment was too sacred. They must only remember the Power, give thanks for victory, ask for safety. Between the pillars of the temple, the fire sprang up towards the darkening sky. The crowd below greeted it with a roar of gratitude, like lions who have triumphed. The Power was on Mount Femarrat; Yadu was safe.

'Time for a drink?' Tekran included both Sarba and Kelith in his smile.

'Why not? I'm too excited to sleep.'

'Have you ever ridden a camel before?'

The three of them turned their steps towards the tavern.

'No! I won't really have to, will I?'

'How else do you think you'll get to Xerappo?'

'Won't there be chariots, or something?'

'That's Ring-Holders for you! Soft. You're riding with the Sorcerer Guard now.'

'But won't I need lessons first? Some practice?'

'Would you like to come down to the barracks now and I'll sign one out? Put you through the basics tonight?' He laughed at her alarmed face and squeezed her arm. 'Only joking. The sentries are as twitchy as a cat on hot stones at the moment. Not a hope of letting one loose after dark. Don't worry; if you don't know how to ride a camel when we set out, you certainly will by the time we get to the Mount of Lemon Trees.'

Sarba was suddenly, sharply, aware of the little letter in the fold of her robe. The Mount of Lemon Trees. Jentiz Yekhavu's colony.

'Unless I fall off and have to be invalided back here,' she joked shakily.

They sat round a table under the stars. It was strange to think this would be the last time for who knew how long. Where would she be tomorrow night? All her life, she had never slept anywhere else but on Mount Femarrat. Those first few years in the family quarters of Cozuman's house, then school and latterly the Ring-Holders' hostel.

Tekran sat looking down at the tankard he was nursing in his hands. 'She looked frightened the other night, didn't she?' he said quietly.

'Who?' asked Kelith.

'Alalia.'

There was an uncomfortable silence.

Then Kelith yawned, a little too widely. 'I don't want to be a spoilsport, but shouldn't you two be getting some sleep? You've got an early start in the morning.'

'By the look of it, you're the one who can't stand the pace,' Tekran teased her. The smile had returned to his face. 'They breed the Sorcerer Guard tougher than that.'

Sarba looked from one to the other of them, her friends. Kelith's long, lovely face, which made her look more serious than she really was. Tekran's crinkling into a ready smile, which masked his reputation as a promising sorcerer.

The edge of the folded paper pressed against her skin. It was a tiny, light thing to feel such a heavy burden. She longed suddenly to share the decision with someone. Should she tell them? Could she trust them?

Out of all the people on Mount Femarrat, out of all the Children of Yadu anywhere, the sparrow had brought this dangerous letter to her. Why? What was so special about her, Sarba Cozuman?

You *are* special, a little voice inside her whispered. After all, only two Ring-Holders were chosen for this mission, out of scores, and you were one. You're the High Sorcerer's only child. Perhaps this is something only you can do.

But *what* must I do? I can't deliver it to him, can I? The father of a traitor? What's inside it?

Her fingers itched to draw the letter out and break the seal.

And why didn't the sparrow take it straight to Jentiz Yekhavu? Why bring it to Sarba, of all people?

'I think Sarba's asleep already.' Tekran nudged her, so that she started back into consciousness of her surroundings. 'Kelith's right. Big day tomorrow. I can't wait to see what it's like on the other side of the border.'

'Xerappan country,' Kelith said, rising. 'You'll need to watch yourselves. You won't be welcome there.'

'They'd be fools to mess with the Sorcerer Guard.'

It should have been a reassurance. Tekran was a tall, warm, solid presence beside her. She would be surrounded by

63

sorcerers on this expedition, armed with spell-rods. So why did she feel their threat was somehow to her as well? Was it because of this little, hidden letter?

Tekran parted from them at the hostel. With a sudden pang, Sarba realized it was too late now to share her secret with him. There was just a short flight of steps and a corridor before Kelith left her too. If she told one of her friends, it must be now.

'Kelith, if someone asked you to help someone else in trouble... if they trusted you... but you were afraid that what they wanted you to do was bad, what would you do?'

'Tell Letizal,' said Kelith promptly. 'She's the Chief Ring-Holder. She'd know the right thing to do.'

Of course, that was what a loyal Ring-Holder would say. She and Kelith had both taken their second vows. They were trained to obedience. The safety of Yadu lay in their hands.

But she felt an obscure disappointment, as though that was not what she had wanted to hear. And she was growing more afraid. She had kept the letter too long already. With each hour that passed, she would look more like a traitor.

'If I don't see you in the morning, good luck!' Kelith hugged her impulsively. 'Stay safe.'

And she was gone.

A tremor filled the dark bedroom, shaking Sarba awake. With the discipline schooled into Ring-Holders, she was instantly alert, hoisting herself up on one elbow in her narrow bed. On the small chest beside her, her bracelet pulsed with a coral glow. Sarba's hand closed over it.

Her mind was still catching up with the reflex obedience of her body. She rubbed her eyes. Why was it so dark outside the window, just a few scattered stars in the black square? If it was nearly time for the Morning Circle, shouldn't dawn be colouring the sky?

The knowledge hit with such force that she leaped out of bed. It was today! Today, she was leaving Mount Femarrat, joining the expedition across the border, with a mission to discover the truth about the colony on the Mount of Lemon Trees.

She was washing, putting on her robe and sandals, brushing her hair, while the doubts and excitement chased each other in circles in her head. She hesitated over her cloak, then stuffed it into her bag. The nights were not cold here and the sun would be up soon enough.

She must not be late. She was scared, suddenly, at being the youngest of the nine. What would they do with her if she failed in her duty?

She was halfway to the door before she remembered. And then she was even more scared. That tiny, folded letter, which she had pushed under her pillow last night... She felt a strong temptation to leave it there, to hurry away and forget all about it.

But she knew she couldn't. What if someone came in and found it? How could she explain? How could she defend herself?

Unwillingly, she forced herself to go back and pick it up. It seemed to burn her hand, as if a sorcerer had laid a spell upon it. *Jentiz Yekhavu*. What was she going to do with it? Almost without realizing she had made the decision, she tucked it into the leather pouch on her girdle. Her chin jutted a little more obstinately. She could make up her mind at the Mount of Lemon Trees, when she saw the situation more clearly.

She had wanted to say a last goodbye to Kelith, but she was afraid there was no time now. Her bracelet cast a faint pink light down the stairs. Hania was approaching from the lower corridor. It was a huge relief. Either she wasn't late or they would be late together.

The Six-Ring-Holder gave her a businesslike smile. 'You're ready? Good. They'll be waiting for us at the stables. Look after this.'

She handed Sarba a large flagon, cased in soft leather. 'Oil?' Sarba asked.

'Of course. I'll take care of the portable Stone and copper bowl myself. Probably unnecessary. The Ring-Holders in Xerappo should have everything there to carry out the ceremonies, just as we do here. But I'm not leaving anything to chance.'

Sarba felt awed at the thought of the tiny block of red jasper, and the miniature bowl which could carry the flame of Power, wherever they were. She would not have wanted the responsibility of bearing them.

How would she have felt, carrying those sacred things, with that undeclared letter in her pouch? Would they have struck her down as a traitor?

I haven't done anything wrong yet, she protested. But her silence itself was wrong.

They were outside, and she had judged well. Even the darkness was warm. She did not need her cloak.

Hania did not seem disposed to conversation. She hurried down the road, slightly ahead of Sarba. With the heavy flagon, as well as her travel bag, the younger girl was having difficulty keeping up.

'Allow me.'

She started, astonished that she had been so full of her own whirling thoughts that she had not heard him coming. Tekran leaned down from his greater height and relieved her of the flagon. 'Jumping camels! That's heavy. What is it?'

'Cedarwood oil, in case we need it to light the flame.'

There was a pause. Sarba sensed a withdrawal of the warmth she usually felt in Tekran's company. 'Of course. I sometimes forget you're a Ring-Holder.'

It hurt. She knew too well what he meant. At fourteen, she had taken the vows to dedicate herself only to the Power of the temple. She would never marry. Last month, she had confirmed those vows. If she had been a sorcerer, there would have been no such barrier between them. Sorcerers married.

They reached the bottom of the hill in an uncomfortable silence. Lights blazed along the perimeter Fence. Another cluster burned at the end of a side street of black cobbles. There were already figures moving there.

'Here you are. Excuse me.' With a swift movement, Tekran handed back the oil and strode ahead. He was a sorcerer on duty.

'Have you ridden a camel before?' Sarba asked Hania.

'Yes, but not often.' She turned to the girl with a brief smile. 'Don't worry. You won't have to do much. Just sit there and hold on. It's not that difficult. But I won't pretend it's comfortable.'

She led Sarba where the lights were brightest. Most of the sorcerers were there. Gordoz, with his lieutenant Undiliz, the woman Innerta and the tall, silent figure of Vendel. Sarba thought he managed to look like a pillar of darkness even under the lamps. Plump Sergeant Ilian was busying himself with a row of kneeling camels. He looked boyishly happy with this responsibility. Six sorcerers, two Ring-Holders. Sarba tried to think who was missing.

'Ah, there you are, ladies. I've picked out a couple of sensible beasts for you. Madam, if you'd take Silver, here. She's a beauty, isn't she?' In the yellow glare of the lights, the grey-white camel looked more like gold. 'And you, miss. I gather you've never ridden before. But don't you worry. I'll see you're all right. Amber here's as steady as a rock.'

Sarba looked with trepidation at the sandy-brown camel kneeling in front of her. Even with its long legs folded beneath it, it looked alarmingly big. When it turned its head towards her, its eyelashes were disarmingly long and curled, but its yellow teeth were ugly.

'Where do I sit?'

'I usually recommend the saddle,' he chuckled.

She felt even more of a fool. Rather too high on the camel's humped back there was indeed a leather saddle, with wooden pommels fore and aft, buckled over a striped rug. But Ilian's laughter was kindly. He had taken charge of her.

'Stow your gear away first. You'll find saddlebags either side, or you can strap stuff on behind.' He made no attempt to do it for her, for which she was grateful. She must learn to look after herself.

'Now, I'll help you up, the first time. But you'll soon get the hang of it. Look, Lady Hania's up already, and I doubt she's ridden a camel more than a few times.' He cupped his hands and hoisted her on to what felt like the mountainside of Amber's hump. She grabbed at the pommel to steady herself, then tried to arrange her skirts discreetly. She felt very exposed.

The sergeant patted Amber's head. 'There's a good boy. Hup, now.'

The beast emitted a strangled roar and lurched forward. For a moment, Sarba thought she would pitch over its head. Then its forelegs straightened to match its back ones. Sarba swayed sickeningly back, then forward. But the jerking steadied. She was sitting aloft, terrifyingly high above the ground.

'Very good, miss. We'll have you cantering in no time.'

'I hope not!' Sarba gasped, clinging on.

'I'll keep close beside you, to start with. But no need really. He's not given to tantrums, that one, unlike some.'

'I'm all right,' she said through stiff lips. 'If you've got other things to do…' She tried to sound braver than she felt.

'We're just about ready,' he said, glancing along the line, where most of the sorcerers were now mounted. 'We're travelling light, this time. Just personal baggage. No extra camels for luggage and camping gear. Not like a real desert expedition. If we get a good pace going, we'll be there tonight.'

She let her own gaze stray along the line of camels and riders. The first hint of dawn was beginning to pale the sky. She could pick out the tall, athletic figure of Tekran, on a darkish animal. A disappointment twisted her heart. Last night, Tekran had joked about taking her down to the camel lines, giving her a first, private lesson in riding a camel. It could have been his hands hoisting her into the saddle, his promise, not Ilian's, to ride alongside her. But she was a Ring-Holder and Tekran had other tasks. They could ride in the same caravan on this mission, but they could never be close.

She must make do with this friendly sergeant, with his fatherly air.

Fatherly... She gulped at the word. She had never known a father like that.

As if summoned by her thought, a chill voice stilled everyone and brought those sorcerers who were on their feet to rigid attention.

'So, Colonel. You're ready to go?'

'Yes, my lord.' Gordoz saluted. 'We were only waiting for Examiner Orzad.'

Sarba straightened her head from the bow she had rather dangerously attempted from the camel's back as soon as she heard her father's voice. The broad face of the Examiner was smiling beside the sharp features of the High Sorcerer. Orzad did not seem hurried or anxious, though he was by far the latest of the expedition to arrive. He must, she thought, have been in conference with Lord Cozuman. It was not by accident they had arrived together. She tried to register the fear that should have caused her. Examiner Orzad was clearly in a different category from the rest of them. He was her father's eyes and ears on this mission. What had Cozuman been saying to him, away from all the others?

Yet, looking at him, it was hard to summon up the same awe her father's presence effortlessly commanded from everyone. The Examiner seemed relaxed, genial.

'Is Beryl ready for me?'

'Ready and waiting, sir.'

The sorcerer walked along the line to his kneeling camel. Unhurriedly, he stowed his travelling case and hoisted himself into the saddle. The last beast rose. The line of nine was complete.

Lord Cozuman stood watching them, his face unreadable.

'Sorcerers and Ring-Holders,' he said gravely, 'Mount Femarrat is in danger. The Children of Yadu are in danger. I look to you to put an end to it.'

There was silence from the nine. The bustle of preparation, the excitement of the expedition, dropped away from them. They were not ordinary people, this was no ordinary mission. The High Sorcerer trusted them.

Sarba longed suddenly for her father to look at her, for his eyes to tell her he had chosen her specially, that he believed in her. It did not happen.

Gordoz lifted his hand in a salute. 'Trust us, my lord. We know what you want.'

Suddenly, Sarba's camel was lurching into movement. The long line was pacing towards the Fence. She was swaying precipitously high above the ground.

In a flash of silver, writhing serpents twisting in columns to left and right, the Fence parted for them. The camels snarled as they felt the force of spells on both sides, but the sorcerers urged them steadily forward into the grey twilight before sunrise.

After a few terrified moments, Sarba realized she was probably not going to fall off just yet. She still gripped the pommel hard, but she could start to look around her. The road led straight across the plain. Against the lightening sky she could see the march of hills which marked the border with Xerappo. Beyond that was alien, enemy country.

Chapter Seven

Three shadowy figures trudged across the grey scrubland. Three livelier jerboas bounded in front of them. Suddenly the sky behind them began to flame. Moments later, the horizon ahead was shot with gold and rose.

The travellers stopped and looked at each other questioningly. Dawn showed a tall, fair girl, her face drawn with weariness, a stocky, broad-shouldered young man with curly black hair, sweat glistening on his grim brow, and a dark girl smaller than either of them, whose jutting chin defied the message her tired legs were sending her.

'Is it safe to go on by daylight?' the fair girl asked.

As if in answer, there was a flutter of wings around her head. She flinched away, but the small brown bird alighted on the sandy ground in front of her. She saw another do the same to Novan, and a third to Mina.

The jerboas stopped. They sat bolt upright, as if listening to the sparrows twitter.

A thought came into Alalia's mind. With a thrill, she realized it came from the brown-and-white jerboa looking up at her.

'They say, make for that hut over there, between the olive trees.'

She turned to the others, and saw that the same thought had sounded in their minds. They were all looking to the north-west, at a low building crouched in the shadow of trees. It might almost have been mistaken for a rock.

There were no paths, no sign of farming or habitation. The olive trees could have been wild.

The sparrows flew ahead. The humans and jerboas followed.

A shadow detached itself from the door of the hut. A man came forward. He wore a brown woollen robe. A yellow scarf hid most of his face.

His voice spoke the smile they could not see. 'Welcome to freedom!'

Dark-haired little Mina looked around her at the barren landscape. She gulped. 'Is this it? Is this where we're going to live?'

The stranger laughed. 'No. We can do better for you than that.'

He led them round the hut. In the shade of the olive trees, three camels rested, their long legs tucked beneath them. Their jaws continued to chew rhythmically as they turned their long necks to stare at the newcomers. They were already saddled.

'One each?' said Alalia nervously. 'I've never ridden a camel on my own before.'

'They will obey your jerboas. You only have to think what you want them to do.'

He helped her into the saddle. The other two were already mounting. The three jerboas hopped up on to the saddles in front of them.

At a word from the man, the camels rose swaying, towering over the little sparrows at their feet.

'You'll find food and water in your saddlebags. Eat while you ride.'

'Won't the sorcerers see us?' asked Mina, looking out across the open desert beyond the trees. 'There's nowhere to hide.'

'The Sorcerer Guard have never come this far, yet.'

The camels were beginning to lurch forward. The flock of

*birds took wing, out from the grey shadows, over the gold
sand.*

*'Where are we going?' Novan asked, turning to look back
at the stranger.*

*His dark eyes gleamed through the folds of his yellow
headscarf.*

'Follow the sparrows.'

As sunrise approached, Mount Femarrat dwindled behind the
sorcerers and Ring-Holders. When Sarba turned her head, she
could only glimpse it through the jacaranda and palm trees
which lined the road. It was unsettling to be leaving it. All her
life had been spent there. How far could its protection reach?

It's not the mountain which protects us, she told herself.
It's the Power we call on there. And that can be anywhere,
even the other side of the border.

It could, couldn't it?

There was no cloud in the sky, but veils of dust were
turning to gold and rose.

Hania urged her camel closer to Colonel Gordoz's.
'Colonel, it's nearly sunrise.'

'Right you are, madam.' He called out to the line of riders,
his voice surprisingly loud and ringing. 'Form the Circle.'

Sarba looked at Sergeant Ilian for help. Was she going to
have to dismount? How?

But the sorcerers nudged their camels towards each other,
so that the beasts formed a ring, with their heads facing
inwards. Ilian struck Amber across his hindquarters, and
Sarba's mount jolted into the formation beside the sergeant's
own camel.

Sarba spoke across the narrowing gap to Hania, 'Do you
need the oil?'

'Don't be silly, girl. We're still in sight of Mount Femarrat.
That flame in the temple is strong enough for the whole land.'

74

The sorcerers reached out their hands on either side. The Ring-Holders did the same. Fingers met. The Circle was formed. On one side of Sarba was the sergeant, on the other, Hania. Tekran was separated from her across the ring, his face towards Femarrat. They waited in silence. Then Sarba saw Tekran's head shoot up, light in his eyes. She twisted her head. On the summit of Mount Femarrat a pillar of red flame soared to the sky through the black columns of the temple.

'Praise be!' Hania cried.

'Praise be! Yadu is safe,' they all responded.

Sarba gazed, entranced. She had never seen it like this, from the plain. She watched the great flame subside, knowing how it would still be flickering in the copper bowl on the red jasper Stone. Other Ring-Holders would be there, at the Great Circles of Morning, Noon and Evening. Kelith would be there, helping to call up that flame, as Sarba herself had only yesterday. A warm wave of pride rose up through her. This was what they did, the Ring-Holders. They kept Yadu safe.

The column of camels was re-forming. The caravan was under way again. As the sun climbed higher, the heat intensified. The sorcerers put on smoked glasses. The individuality of their faces was reduced. Five men and one woman in red uniforms. Only Orzad wore robes like the two Ring-Holders.

'Did you remember to put your sun-cream on?' Hania turned her head to ask Sarba.

'No! I forgot.' Blushing with more than the sun's heat, she bent down and fumbled in her saddlebag, hoping a sudden lurch from her camel wouldn't pitch her over its side. She pulled a loose fold of her robe up over her head, and rubbed the protective ointment into her bare arms and face. It occurred to her with a sudden pleasure that she had let go of the pommel without falling off.

Something was happening up ahead. Gordoz pulled his camel to a halt and lifted his hand for the others to stop. Sarba was aware that Sergeant Ilian had manœuvred his mount alongside hers and was peering intently forward.

A cloud of dust was approaching rapidly. Yet whatever was throwing it up was no ordinary group of travellers. Out of the dust shot red lightnings. The sorcerers drew their spell-rods. Slender white cylinders, tipped with gold, pointed steadily towards the oncoming storm.

'Oh, I don't think there's any need for weapons.' The measured, almost amused, voice of Examiner Orzad sounded from behind Sarba. 'They must be ours. Only sorcerers could put on such an impressive display. A little self-indulgent, perhaps.'

The dust cloud was bearing down fast on the stationary caravan. Now they could see that at its centre was a knot of horsemen. Red uniforms proclaimed that they were from the Sorcerer Guard. The lightning flashes shot from a single figure in the lead. One hand gripped his horse's reins. The other brandished his spell-rod in what looked like fury.

As the gap closed, Sarba gasped, 'Digonez!'

The name ran through the waiting group as the approaching horsemen reined in to a skidding halt.

Sarba gazed at her cousin in awe. His handsome face was glistening with sweat. White spittle foamed on his lips. His grey eyes flashed fury almost as brilliantly as the sparks still cascading from his spell-rod.

'Foolish. He'll exhaust himself, if he keeps that up,' Orzad murmured. 'Magic needs to be used sparingly.'

'What news, Lieutenant?' Colonel Gordoz was superior in rank to Digonez, but his tone conveyed the respect they all felt towards the High Sorcerer's nephew.

Digonez lowered his spell-rod. The dust cloud began to settle, shrouding the red uniforms with gold. He spat the words out. 'The traitor Balgo Yekhavu is dead.'

'We knew that before we left Mount Femarrat, the Power

forgive him.' Fury blazed up again in Digonez's eyes, but the colonel went on steadily, 'Balgo wore the High Sorcerer's bracelet. I see you have it now.' His eyes went to a band of silver on Digonez's wrist, in which a purple stone burned darkly. 'Lord Cozuman knew when it changed hands, and why.'

'Yes. I killed him. And with good reason.'

'And the girl. Did you get Alalia Yekhavu?' The usually withdrawn, taciturn sorcerer Vendel leaned forward with abnormal eagerness.

Digonez met his eyes, as if they shared a common intention. 'There was sorcery there, and it was used against the Children of Yadu. I'm sure she and her Xerappan cronies were in that valley. But if they were, we couldn't see them. I threw a ring of demons round them, but still they escaped!' His voice was rising, the flashes from his spell-rod spitting in all directions. Orzad muttered a spell of protection and Sarba saw something shimmer across the road between the two groups.

'Hmm. Maybe I was a little premature about our need of defence.'

Sarba looked at the Examiner in astonishment. How could he seem so relaxed, so humorous, when everyone knew the danger of Digonez's rages? And didn't he grieve that their friend Balgo was dead?

Digonez was struggling to master himself. 'I have at least got *these* for the High Sorcerer. A dozen Xerappan rebels, captured in their hideout, like rats in a trap. He's going to enjoy questioning them.'

The rage of this tall, arrogant sorcerer had made it almost impossible to look at anything else. But now everyone was staring beyond him, as the knot of his guards fell back to show their prisoners.

Xerappans, roped to the tails of the sorcerers' horses. Their chests heaved with the punishing pace they had been forced to run. Their dark heads hung with weariness, or fear. Two of them must have collapsed, because each was slung over the pillion of a sorcerer's mount, his wrists and ankles lashed together under the horse's belly.

Sarba felt fear herself, looking at these men. These were the enemies of her country. These were the rebels the Yadu must always guard against. The old inhabitants of the land, who could not accept that the war was lost and still claimed that this land was theirs. The border Fence was meant to keep them out. Those Xerappans who had remained in Yadu were cowed, obedient, since that terrible day when Sarba's mother had been poisoned. Nothing like it had ever happened again. Her father had made sure of that. But these dangerous men had been caught inside the border Fence. Suddenly, the Children of Yadu had become vulnerable again.

'On your way then, Lieutenant. We won't detain you.' Gordoz skilfully manœuvred his camel backwards to let the horsemen and their prisoners pass.

Digonez started to move on. Then he stopped his horse abruptly. 'Where are you bound for?'

Colonel Gordoz looked back down the line at Orzad, as if for permission. When the Examiner nodded, he answered, 'The Mount of Lemon Trees. Balgo Yekhavu's father is governor there. Your uncle thinks he may have useful information.'

'Jentiz Yekhavu? The local sorcerers have questioned him, haven't they? They've certainly dealt with the Xerappan runaways' family.'

'Nevertheless, the High Sorcerer feels more... skilled... enquiries might be profitable.'

Was that menace now, under the Examiner's smooth voice? Was Sarba included in that 'skill'?

Digonez came on, followed by his sorcerers and their

captives. Sarba tried to work out how the others had guided their camels backwards out of the way. Amber refused to budge.

Her cousin's horse was alongside her camel now. His eyes suddenly looked up and caught her face. 'Sarba? What in the name of all the demons are *you* doing here?'

It was startling to realize that, perched on Amber's back, she was looking down on tall Digonez for the first time.

'I'm a Ring-Holder. The High Sorcerer chose me.' She was surprised by the cold steadiness of her voice.

'Your father? It's not like him to give way to sentiment.'

'I think Lord Cozuman knows talent when he sees it.' Orzad had moved his mount silently level with hers. He murmured a word, and both beasts shuffled a few paces back off the road.

Sarba watched as Digonez's party filed past her. The sorcerers with him looked exhausted too. A battle conducted by magic is every bit as draining as the conventional sort. And the Sorcerer Guard had failed in their main objective. Apparently, Alalia Yekhavu and her Xerappan companions were still free. Sarba's heart leaped in her throat at the thought. Was it fear of them, or something more irrational?

She had little compassion for the beaten Xerappans, dragged behind the horses' tails. They would have killed her, wouldn't they? Only one, a larger man than all the rest, lifted his head defiantly as he passed, and stared straight into her face. His dark eyes made her shudder. No, she thought, he's not beaten yet. But he hasn't met my father.

Examiner Orzad's camel paced beside hers. Their gait seemed unhurried, but their long, swinging legs ate up the miles. The ground was rising. The lush green of orchards and fields was running out, giving way to sandy slopes and bare rock. Sarba looked up. The hills seemed more formidable, now that they towered above her. Somewhere up there must be the border Fence.

'I expect this is your first time across the border.' The Examiner's voice broke the silence.

'Yes, I hardly go outside Mount Femarrat… except to visit my mother.'

'Of course.' She heard the sympathy in his murmur. Everyone knew her story, though few spoke about it. 'I don't imagine you've conducted an investigation before.'

'No.'

You knew that, too, she thought. You'll have examined my file at Headquarters before this expedition set out. All of our files. You probably know things about me I don't even know myself.

Does Orzad know about the sparrow and the letter? *Could* he?

'If I may offer a word of advice, I find, myself, that a sympathetic questioner often gets the best results.' She heard the smile in his voice, but she dared not look at him. 'It encourages the interviewee to relax, let down their guard. But the prisoner can sense if it's a sham. You need to enter imaginatively into their situation, see it from their point of view. If you were in their shoes, what would *you* do? Of course, once the interview is over, you must recover your objectivity immediately and write up your notes, leaving nothing out.' His voice had hardened. She felt him looking keenly at her and could not quite meet his eyes.

'Don't our sorcerers have magic which can make people tell them the truth?'

He sighed. 'You must understand that magic involves a strong element of force. Yes, there are those who like to use coercion.' His gaze went up the column ahead. She guessed he was looking at the erect figure of Vendel, in his dark red tunic, riding silently alongside Sorcerer Innerta. Even Vendel's back view made her shiver.

'The danger is,' he went on, 'that such a sorcerer will

80

compel the prisoner to tell him what he wants to hear. That may not be what is actually true. I find sympathy a more reliable key to unlock the gates of truth.'

This time she could not avoid his smile. It seemed warm, genuine. There was nothing sinister about his broad, blunt face. She was seized with a sudden longing to tell him everything about the letter, to ask his advice.

The moment was broken as Innerta turned in her saddle and called back to them, 'Lunch stop.'

The leaders were already swinging their camels off the road to the open gate of a large wayside inn. Date palms offered welcome shade after the bare rocks of the hillside. There was the tinkle of a fountain.

Now, thought Sarba, I have to get off.

Before Sergeant Ilian could help her, a quiet word from Orzad brought both their camels to their knees. Sarba clung on, to prevent herself being pitched head first to the ground. But it was over. She was at ground level again. She could dismount, almost gracefully. She allowed herself to pat Amber, cautiously. He turned his long-lashed eyes to her.

She heard Hania call her. The two Ring-Holders and the sorcerer Innerta were shown inside the cool building to refresh themselves.

She could catch Hania alone now and tell her. But it was becoming ever more difficult. How could she explain why she had waited so long to confess? Hania, she knew, would report it straight to the Colonel and the Examiner. It would not be long before the message got back to the High Sorcerer.

It was already impossible.

They rejoined the men at a table in a courtyard shaded by vines. There was cheese and olives, and melon juice to drink.

Sarba's eyes travelled up the last slopes to the brilliant blue sky. What she saw was a shock, almost as if she had been caught in the spell itself.

The silver mesh dazzled, so that she could hardly look at it. Even from this far beneath, it looked enormous. The border Fence. The last barrier between Yadu and Xerappo.

'In a few more hours, we'll be across the border, in unknown territory.' It was Tekran, on the other side of Hania, catching her eye. He must have seen her face and known what she was thinking.

'Not as unknown as all that,' said Hania. 'We get regular reports from the colonies. I've visited several of them myself.'

This mission is routine, just a job, Sarba told herself. But she knew from the way the sorcerers were talking quietly to each other, the underlying tension in the air, that, this time, it was more than that.

As they crested the ridge, Sarba fought not to be overawed by the Fence. It's only its size, she thought. It can't be more powerfully spelled than the Fence guarding Mount Femarrat.

'Lord Cozuman's mission to the Mount of Lemon Trees,' said Colonel Gordoz to the guards.

He presented his papers. If he had thought the High Sorcerer's name would mean they were waved through without formalities, he was mistaken. The sentries were on edge. Alalia Yekhavu's party must have passed through here, only a few days ago, coming into Yadu for her betrothal, thought Sarba. Is she still here on this side, somewhere in these hills, hiding? Surely, no one could break through this Fence back into Xerappo, alive?

But those Xerappans Digonez had captured had got into Yadu.

They had to dismount and be searched by the sentries' spell-rods. As she waited her turn to be checked by the guards, Sarba strained to see ahead, but the towering Fence blocked the road. Though it was made of open, silvery mesh, she could not look at it steadily enough to see through it. Again, those serpents writhed, heaved, along its wires. They heaped themselves over and around each other, as in a snake pit. It was too threatening, too terrifying, to watch. What happened if someone touched that Fence, or tried to cut it? Would they be felled instantly, scorched to ashes by the spell? Or would those coiling serpents break loose all around them? She felt faint at the thought.

She was at the head of the queue now. Could the sentries probing her with their rods feel how her heart was racing? She had almost forgotten about the letter in her pouch. She attempted a placating smile at the guard searching her. It brought no answering softness to the set of his jaw. These sorcerers felt responsible for what had happened. They all did. The High Sorcerer's fury hung like a thundercloud over the whole land. It would not lift until they found the truth and captured the fugitives.

Could I do that? Sarba thought. Could I play a part? Would my father love me if I did?

'Move, Ring-Holder Cozuman!' Colonel Gordoz's voice recalled her to reality. The sorcerer who had searched her was looking impatient. Tekran was still behind her. Ilian was coming towards her, leading her camel.

It was over. She had passed the test. Nobody suspected her. Blushing with confusion, she remounted Amber.

As he rose to his full height, the Fence shuddered. The serpents grew still. They seemed to fade slowly, to shrink back into the silvery wires. The Fence was folding aside, glittering panels doubling back on each other, clearing the way ahead. She felt a shudder run through Amber, too. No animal liked to pass through the concentrated magic of a Fence.

'Steady, boy, it's all right.' She tried to speak to him soothingly, as she had heard Ilian do. He gave a low roar, lifted his head with dignity and paced on. They were through, and the barrier was closing behind them.

Suddenly, she could see in front of her. The ground fell away down the hillside. Bare screes, roped with silver cables, on either side of the road. She was sure they held more protective magic, to warn of anyone trying to creep up off the road. Below was a land like nothing she had seen before: brown, patched with little fields of vegetation, so not quite a desert. Her heart ached for the brilliant, fertile green of the Plain of Yadu behind her. Her eyes were drawn to a few oases of familiar colour. All round a brown and grey-green valley stood a ring of hills clad in brighter green. Proud on their flattened peaks, colonies of white houses flashed in the sun. She even thought she caught the wink of a swimming pool.

Gordoz pointed across the valley with his spell-rod. 'The Mount of Lemon Trees.'

'Civilization!' laughed Tekran. 'I'm dying for a shower and a swim.'

Sarba turned her head to him. Is that what it would be like? A miniature Mount Femarrat? As familiar as home?

The camels started to sway down the steep path. They were approaching a hairpin bend. The firm road of the Yadu side had given way to stones and dirt. Sarba looked ahead down the slope, hoping that Amber could pick his way accurately over this looser footing.

There was something brown at the hairpin bend. It was shifting, moving. Was the hillside starting to give way? Were those stones rolling down, gathering into an avalanche?

She gave a start that almost made her fall off her saddle. Those were not stones, hopping at the edge of the road. It was a little flock of sparrows. She stared intently, but not one of them showed a glint of gold ribbon on its leg. They seemed just sparrows, the commonest of birds. So familiar, people hardly noticed them.

Yet as Amber carried her nearer to them, an excited twittering broke out. The birds rose in a cloud before her, as if they had only been waiting for her to arrive. There was a commotion of wings in front of her face. Then the flock took off, over the edge of the mountain into the blue air. She watched them dwindle across the valley below. Some of them were making for the Mount of Lemon Trees, but the rest broke away and flew out towards the distant desert.

Chapter Eight

It was not like Mount Femarrat. They came to it across a dusty valley, with ruined buildings, which Sarba supposed must have belonged to the missing Xerappans' family. A trail of smoke rose from one pile of rubble, as though someone was still camping out there. Goats moved between the shadows of scattered olive trees, looking for thin grass and straggling weeds.

There was no Fence around the base of the Mount of Lemon Trees. The colony's orchards and vegetable fields flowed down the slopes. They were clearly well watered and carefully tended. The contrast with Femarrat was striking. The vivid green of the lemon-tree leaves could hardly be more different from the pure white rock of the sacred mountain.

Two sorcerers patrolled the foot of the hill. Their epaulettes showed them to be of junior rank. Though they were clearly on edge, they seemed in awe of this mission from the High Sorcerer, unlike those at the border Fence. They inspected, somewhat awkwardly, Colonel Gordoz's papers, then waved the party past without searching them.

The Fence was higher up. As they climbed the hill, Sarba was suddenly aware how tired and hot she was. As Tekran rode level with her, she threw him a rueful smile.

'I never realized how exhausting it would be, just sitting in a saddle all day. I'm aching in muscles I didn't even know I had.'

'You've done well, though. You haven't fallen off once.'

'Did you think I would?'

'You might have, if we'd had to break into a gallop.'

'Do camels gallop?' It was an alarming thought.

'Surely you know they have camel races? Not that I think your… what's he called?'

'Amber.'

'… Amber would win any prizes. He's not exactly the world's most streamlined animal, is he?'

'He's fine for me. Steady.'

'Exactly. Not like Basalt.' He leaned over and patted the neck of his own dark mount. Basalt had, Sarba thought, a wicked look in his eye. She felt a rush of gratitude to Sergeant Ilian for not giving her a high-mettled camel like that. She was feeling almost affectionate towards her own mount now.

'Have you raced him?' She had a vision of Tekran, on his magnificent beast, whirling across the plain in a sandstorm of flying hooves, with the crowd yelling him on.

'Sorcerer Tekran, I think we need to have a few words.' Orzad's voice cut in from behind them. He did not raise it. Did Sarba only imagine she heard an edge to it?

She fell instantly silent, as if she had been scolded.

'Yes, sir,' said Tekran. Blushing slightly, the tall young sorcerer reined back to fall in with the Examiner.

They were coming to the place where the colony's Fence blocked the road. It was, Sarba saw, not appropriate for the two of them to approach it chattering like any other pair of teenagers. This was a very serious mission. They must bring all the dignity of their office to it. Tekran was a sorcerer. She was a Ring-Holder. Any personal relationship between them was inappropriate. She let her camel catch up with Hania, who was waiting for her.

There were more sorcerer sentries on the other side of the wire. There was a brilliant shimmer in the air. Two of them suddenly reappeared outside the Fence. It made Sarba shiver, because she had not been able to see how it happened.

This time, the checks were more thorough. They were searched with spell-rods. The words of power, which she could hardly bear to hear, were spoken, and the Fence shuddered aside. She must not look at it. But out of the corner of her eye she could not help seeing the flicker of serpents as she passed.

They paced up the main avenue, under the welcome shade of trees. Fair-haired Yadu children were playing in the gardens of spacious houses. The occasional shout of laughter rang out. The children, at least, did not realize the calamity that had befallen this place.

There were some Xerappans too, servants, she supposed. The sight of these squat, dark people brought the familiar wave of revulsion.

'Company, dismount,' Colonel Gordoz called.

Could it be true, they were really here? Was it only the day before yesterday that she had woken up, in her little bedroom in the hostel on Mount Femarrat, with no idea that today she would ride a camel over the hills into another country, that she would be part of the High Sorcerer's mission? She was working with at least one sorcerer, she was certain, who ranked high in her father's secret command. As she tumbled off Amber, rather less gracefully this time, she was not sure whether she felt more proud or scared by this.

The camels were being led off to the stables. Someone handed her her luggage, which she had almost forgotten. On an impulse, she turned back. Her hand traced the curve of Amber's hairy neck.

'Goodbye, and thank you.'

He snorted what sounded like a colossal sneeze.

'I'll show you where you're sleeping.'

There was a girl beside her. She was a Ring-Holder, Sarba realized with a start. Her glance flew to the hem of the girl's skirt. Two rings, like her own. She raised her eyes and smiled.

'Hello. I'm Sarba.'

'I'm Letti. What's that you've got, besides your travel bag?'

'Oil. Hania said we had to bring everything we needed to make a Circle: a portable Stone, a copper bowl, oil.' She caught the outraged look on Letti's face and laughed. 'Yes, I know. I'm sorry. I'm sure you've got everything here.'

'We may live on the wrong side of the border and out of sight of Mount Femarrat, but we're not exactly a bunch of savages here, you know.'

'I'm sure you're not. Hania just wanted to be prepared for any emergency.'

'We have sorcerers and Ring-Holders here, and we can call on the other colonies. I think we can handle any emergencies, thank you... In here.'

They turned off the street into the garden of a small one-storeyed house. Letti led the way between oleander bushes. There were voices inside.

Hania was standing talking to an older woman, another Ring-Holder. Sarba quickly counted her rings. Five. So Hania was one ring senior to her.

'Welcome to the Mount of Lemon Trees. Sarba, is it? I'm Vazia. I see you and Letti are getting to know one another. You'll be comfortable enough with us. I expect you're dying for supper. I remember when I was a growing girl your age, I could eat the men under the table!'

Sarba was slightly shocked. There was a dignity about Letizal and Hania and the other senior Ring-Holders on Mount Femarrat. They did not joke with the younger ones. And Vazia was unusually heavily built for a Daughter of Yadu. Sarba was used to women who were tall and slender. The diet at the Ring-Holders' hostel was frugal.

'Just drop your bag in Letti's room. Food's nearly ready.'

It took a few moments for the words to register in Sarba's mind. Her eyes flew to Letti, but the other girl was already leading the way out of the living room. There was a corridor, and then a smaller room, with a window opening on to the leafy back garden. There was a bed, clearly Letti's. Another, narrower, one had been squeezed in against the opposite wall. Letti was already setting down Sarba's bag on it.

'I'm sharing with you?' Sarba asked stupidly. It was obviously true.

'You don't mind, do you?' The other girl's narrow face suddenly looked worried. 'We do have a guest house, but with so many visitors, we've turned that over to your men. Vazia thought you and your boss would be happier with us. She's all right, Vazia, really. She's quite a laugh. But if you're not happy… maybe somebody else has a spare room.'

'No, no, it's all right. It's really kind of you.'

It was years since she had shared a room with anyone else. Particular friendships were not encouraged among Ring-Holders, though they happened. Sarba treasured her privacy. As she tried to smile politely, she was suddenly seized with a worse anxiety. If she was never alone, even at night, how could she take out that little letter in her pouch and decide what to do with it?

Her fears were interrupted by a tap on the door. Vazia put her face round with a rueful laugh.

'Letti, I'll be forgetting my head next. Why didn't you remind me? With all this excitement, I nearly forgot the Evening Circle. Hania had to remind me. Come on, it's time.'

Sarba stared at her, shocked. How was it possible that a senior Ring-Holder could forget one of the three vital ceremonies of the day? This was what Ring-Holders were *for*. Their whole lives were dedicated to calling on the Power which kept the Children of Yadu safe. And then the voice of conscience whispered in her head: *You forgot it too. You didn't notice how the sun was going down. You can't rely on the Mount Femarrat system out here.*

90

Vazia turned to her. 'You'll join us tonight, won't you, Sarba? You've no idea what it's like, just the two of us Ring-Holders to do everything by ourselves. Of course, it's not every week. We only light one flame for all the colonies in Xerappo. Each colony takes its turn. It's the Mount of Lemon Trees this week.'

She chattered away as she led them across the back garden to a grassy mound.

'In the first place, we tried just holding hands in a circle, as they do across Yadu when you light the flame on Mount Femarrat. But somehow, this side of the border, it didn't seem enough to maintain the magic. We need to call down the Power for ourselves. So each colony has a High Place, and Ring-Holders to keep it.'

There were steps up the mound. Sarba drew in her breath. It was a miniature of the temple on Mount Femarrat, pared down to its bare essentials. No roof, no black pillars. A circular platform, chalk-white. Four black boulders, one at each point of the compass. And at the centre, a block of red jasper and a copper bowl. They were far smaller than the ones on Mount Femarrat, but they still sent a thrill through her. These were things of Power.

There was no wall round the platform. She was looking straight out across the land of Xerappo. The dry valley far below, the ring of hills, each with a new town on the summit and a clothing of greenery around its slopes. And between the hills, a glimpse of the desert.

A sorcerer had come up the steps behind them, a man of her father's generation. Tall, fair, lean-faced, like so many others. Rather serious in expression beside Vazia's plump cheerfulness. Sarba's tired mind was beginning to swim with all these new impressions. How could she read the minds of so many strangers?

Letti picked up a horn from one of the boulders. She blew

it, with notes whose daily familiarity sounded all the odder in this alien setting. Sarba had hardly been aware of the sounds of life in the colony around her. But instantly they fell still. The silence was gripping. Everywhere, all across Yadu and in every Yadu colony in Xerappo, there would be this same stillness, at this same moment. She reached out to Letti with one hand and Hania with the other. All the Children of Yadu would be holding hands like this, renewing their commitment to each other, and to the Power. The sorcerer levelled his spell-rod. As the four Ring-Holders raised their hum to a chant, he spoke the word of power. Flame reared from the copper bowl. Sarba expected it to soar for the sky, as it did on Mount Femarrat, higher than the temple. She felt an obscure disappointment, even a touch of alarm. The flame rose hardly higher than Vazia's head, before it settled to a steady glow on the surface of the copper bowl. Was this enough to keep them safe in a hostile country? She looked at Hania, and saw the older woman's lips were drawn together tightly. Did she have doubts too?

Of course, things were smaller, more makeshift here. The land of Xerappo was not wholly theirs yet. But didn't that mean they needed all the more protection?

Are you going to endanger that protection? What are you going to do with that letter?

I can't do anything with it, she told herself. I'd never get a chance to deliver it to Jentiz Yekhavu, even if I wanted to. And I certainly don't.

Just as she thought that, a sparrow flew down and landed in the Circle, on the white floor. It hopped its way towards the Stone, as though untroubled by flame or Power or spell-rods. Sarba watched it, mesmerized.

The interrogations began next morning. The nine from Mount Femarrat met in a room of the guest house to receive their briefings from Colonel Gordoz.

'Orzad, you'll interview Jentiz Yekhavu. That's our top priority. Tekran, you'll go with him and take notes. Hania will question the Ring-Holders.'

Sarba waited for her expected assignment. She would obviously be taking notes for Hania. She was startled when Gordoz went on, 'Sarba, you'll sit in on Jentiz Yekhavu's interrogation too. You need to learn as much as you can from him about Alalia's friends, her background.'

She caught the same surprise in Tekran's face. They exchanged the tiniest of smiles, hardly more than their eyes.

'Vendel and Innerta, you take the sorcerers. That's a big job. In frontier territory, every other adult is a sorcerer. Meanwhile, Undiliz and I will pay those Xerappans' grandparents a social call.' He and his lieutenant exchanged laughs. 'Ilian, you chat to the farm staff. Nothing official, you understand. Hands in pockets. Admire their camels. Ask about the lemon harvest. You know the sort of thing.'

The sergeant grinned. 'Got you, sir.'

A chill went through Sarba. So Sergeant Ilian was more than the bluff, kindly man she had thought him, who had only come along to look after their camels.

Is that what I'm like? Just a teenage girl on the surface. A low-ranking Ring-Holder. Somebody other girls can chat to without suspicion?

Her father had planned the composition of this mission very carefully.

They went out into the dazzling sunshine. The colony's guard post was not far away. Its shadowed interior temporarily blinded Sarba. They were led into a small room. A table with two chairs for Orzad and Tekran, another chair for herself, set more to the side. A single empty chair in front of the table. The walls were plain, pale green. There were bars and a metal mesh over the window. Sarba wondered if it was reinforced with spells.

She had barely seated herself, with her notebook ready on her knee, when there were steps in the corridor. A tap on the half-open door.

'Enter,' called Orzad.

Two sorcerers came into the room, both in the customary dark red uniform. Sarba's eyes went straight to the second one. He might be a prisoner, brought here for interrogation, but Colonel Jentiz Yekhavu was a man who carried authority. He was tall, even for a Son of Yadu. Whatever he felt about the humiliation to which he was being subjected, he carried himself as straight and unyielding as those iron bars on the window. He was still, in his bearing, the governor of this colony. He must have been middle-aged, the father of Balgo and Alalia, but his figure was still lean and trim, and his face would have been handsome if it had not been scored with deep lines of grief.

Seeing the gold epaulettes of a colonel, Sarba instinctively started to rise. Obedience and respect for rank were schooled into Ring-Holders. Then she saw that Examiner Orzad remained seated, though he ranked lower than a colonel. Tekran glanced briefly at Orzad and kept his seat too. Embarrassed, Sarba subsided back into hers. The governor's sorcerer escort stepped discreetly into a corner and stood motionless.

Orzad's own fleshier face smiled up at the colonel. 'Good morning, Jentiz. This is a sad state of affairs.' Jentiz's face stiffened, but he made no answer. 'I see they haven't stripped you of your uniform yet. You still wear a colonel's epaulettes.'

'They've taken my sorcerer's rod. I should like to know why. I'm still governor of this colony. I've done nothing wrong.'

'Just a formality. I'm sure we can straighten this out, with your co-operation. Take a seat.'

For a moment, Sarba thought the governor's pride would

refuse the offer. Then he sat, folding his long limbs awkwardly, unrelaxed.

'My wife? Have you brought her back with you? How is she?'

'Emania is... as well as can be expected. Lord Cozuman thinks it would be better to keep her in his house until this unhappy business is sorted out. She's naturally upset at losing both her son and her daughter in such unfortunate circumstances.'

The Examiner's smile was as warm as ever, but Sarba saw the flash of alarm that passed over Jentiz's face. The stiff formality of his speech burst into urgent pleading. 'What's happened to Alalia? She's not dead too, is she?'

Sarba made her first note on the clean page. *He cares more about Alalia than his wife.*

'That, Jentiz, is what we should all like to know. Your daughter ran away from her betrothal to the High Sorcerer's nephew, with two Xerappans. She not only insulted Lord Cozuman, she escaped from the most tightly guarded stronghold in Yadu. You do not need me to tell you the implications of *that* for national security. We are very interested indeed in finding Alalia.'

Jentiz's face turned white. 'Why come to me? It was as great a shock to me as to everyone else.'

'And yet you didn't come to Mount Femarrat yourself for the betrothal. That, too, *could* be construed as an insult to Lord Cozuman.'

A flush crept over those pale cheeks, deep riven with furrows of grief. 'Lord Cozuman knows why. There were rumours from our Xerappan informers that something really big was going to happen. I couldn't take the risk of leaving the colony at such a time.'

'Something big?' Orzad stroked his double chin. 'Something big *did* happen, but on Mount Femarrat, not here.'

'I tell you, that's as much a mystery to me as to you. Have pity, man! My son's dead and my daughter's been kidnapped.'

'Kidnapped? Now what makes you say that?'

The governor tensed. 'She must have been, mustn't she? She's just a teenager. She hardly knows Yadu and Mount Femarrat. How could she just disappear? Someone must have taken her.'

'Someone did take her. Your son, Balgo.'

There was a shocked silence. Clearly Jentiz Yekhavu had not been told the full story.

'But Balgo... He wouldn't have... He was in his first year as a sorcerer. Alalia's fiancé, Digonez, was his hero.'

'Yet when Digonez caught up with them, Balgo fought a duel of magic against him. He died, of course. But it allowed Alalia to escape.'

'He... did... that? For Alalia?' The muscles of Jentiz's face seemed to have difficulty moving.

'You're not suggesting, I hope, that it was a brave and brotherly act. It was *high treason*.'

The menacing words did not seem to be registering in Jentiz's brain. 'I didn't think he had it in him,' he added softly. 'I underestimated him.'

Tekran, Sarba noted, was writing busily. She wanted to cry out to this honest, grieving man, 'Be careful what you say. It doesn't sound good. It's too late to sympathize with Balgo.'

Jentiz seemed to understand this. He pulled himself up straighter in his chair. 'Forgive me, it's been a great shock. I can't explain any of this. Balgo must have thought he was doing the right thing, but of course it was wrong for a probationer to fight a lieutenant of the High Sorcerer's personal guard.'

Orzad stroked his neck with a long, thoughtful movement. 'The question remains, how could your children possibly have thought that what they were doing was right? ... I believe you've given money to the local school for Xerappan children?'

Sarba saw the start Jentiz gave at this sudden switch of questioning. 'I... It was a private donation. I didn't intend to make it known.'

'No. It was hardly appropriate, was it, for a governor of a Yadu colony? You know that Lord Cozuman's policy is to encourage all Xerappans to leave here.'

'I know that Yadu has to expand. But I can't see us doing away with Xerappans altogether. We need their labour. And since we need some of them to stay, we should treat them humanely.'

'Lord Cozuman would prefer the land without them.'

'Where would they go?'

The Examiner shrugged. 'Into the desert. There are oases, aren't there? Let the Xerappans go there... Now, Alalia's friends. What can you tell us about them?'

This time it was Sarba who was caught by surprise at the abrupt change of subject. She poised her pencil.

Jentiz frowned. 'There's not much to say. I'm a busy man. I don't have much time to listen to girls' gossip. It was the normal thing – clothes, boys. What do you expect me to tell you?'

'I don't think I'm quite getting through to you, Colonel. Your daughter was obviously *not* a normal girl. No normal girl would refuse Lieutenant Digonez for a husband. No normal girl would run away from Mount Femarrat at the cost of her brother's life. No normal girl would elude the entire Sorcerer Guard. *What can you tell us about her friends?*'

'I...' Jentiz swallowed. 'You could try the girl next door. Chelya. She knew her better than anyone else. Teenage girls don't usually share their secrets with their fathers.'

Chelya. Sarba wrote the name carefully. Tomorrow she would need to talk to this girl.

'Did she have Xerappan friends?'

'Of course not!'

'Yet two Xerappans fled with her. They've not yet been captured.'

'I know nothing about them.'

'Let me prompt your memory. Novan, the leopard-driver, and Mina, your daughter's maid.'

'The driver was my wife's choice. She wanted leopards to pull their chariot in Yadu, to make a big impression. The lad was the best cat handler we had. And Mina used to sweep our floors. She was a bright little thing, but she wasn't really Alalia's personal maid, not until a few days ago. But Alalia insisted she needed to take a maid of her own, like her mother. It was a big occasion for the womenfolk, this betrothal. There was no talk of breaking it off.'

Sarba looked at what she had just written without thinking.

Not until she met Digonez again!

Horrified, she covered it with her hand, glancing up to see if Orzad could have read it.

Her eye was caught by a flicker of movement at the window beyond Orzad's head. A little sparrow, hopping on the ledge on the other side of the bars. Her heart skipped a beat. The sparrow was watching her with very bright eyes. It could not get between the bars for the wire mesh.

A fragment of truth fell into place. The pouch carrying the little letter burned against her waist. So the sparrow could not have delivered it to Jentiz Yekhavu in this guard post. But she, Sarba, was inside those bars.

Chapter Nine

Three camels crested the skyline in the rose-pink dawn. The watchers on the city walls tensed. Messengers sped to Rasmullin, Defender of the City, and Gamatea, Guardian of the Pool. They exchanged glances, of fear, of hope.

Rasmullin donned his breastplate and buckled on his sword. Gamatea drew on her feathered cloak. They hurried out to the gate of the Forgotten City.

The strangers were nearing the edge of the oasis. The camels were coming on more swiftly now, lured by the scent of water and vegetation. Their riders swayed with weariness.

Ahead of them, a swirl of brown mist resolved itself into a flock of sparrows, rushing across the fields in a flurry of excited wings. They whirled in front of Gamatea and Rasmullin, dozens of voices cheeping against one another.

'They've come!'

'It's her, isn't it? The one you wanted?'

'A Yadu girl, here in the Forgotten City!'

'There are two Xerappans with her.'

'This must be the one!'

Gamatea held up her hands. The birds stilled. Some settled on her shoulders and arms.

'Peace, my little brothers and sisters. Let me look.'

She gazed at the three camels and riders, now pacing between the fields of melons and date palms. The tallest rider was a slender girl with long fair hair. Her face was drawn with grief and exhaustion. A dark-haired boy, a younger version of the burly Rasmullin, watched her anxiously. Smaller than either of them, a girl with the same curly black hair stared all around her, her eyes bright with curiosity.

Gamatea's face relaxed. 'You have done well, little ones. The fugitives you have brought are indeed a treasure of great price. A Yadu bride and a Xerappan groom, to heal with their love the age-long wounds between our peoples. But she is still to come, who has a greater destiny.'

The birds took off into the air.

'I told you.'

'She kept Black-Bib back, didn't she?'

'A special mission.'

'But where? Who is this other girl?'

Rasmullin turned to Gamatea. Dark eyes, deep with concern, met her unsettling blue. 'You're sure about that other girl? She, of all the Yadu?'

'The risk is very real. But only she can change what must be changed.'

Xerappan guards were hastening out to lead the camels to the city gate. Little children swarmed around the procession, staring up at the first blonde girl they had ever seen.

Gamatea held out her arms. 'Alalia Yekhavu, welcome! You are the first Yadu to enter these gates in a hundred years. Come in, in peace, to the Forgotten City.'

Rasmullin was calling up to Novan. 'Good news, lad! Your family reached us safely.'

'They're here!' Mina tumbled off her camel so fast, she lost her balance and sprawled in the sand. A dozen hands helped her up. The crowd parted. She and Novan were lost in the embrace of the parents they had feared they would never see again.

Alalia watched them, and bit her lip.

There was a touch on her shoulder. Gamatea's blue eyes smiled at her, oddly familiar among all these dark Xerappans.

100

'Do not lose hope. Love may penetrate even your father's prison bars.'

The Mount Femarrat party queued for lunch in the colony's canteen. Instinctively, the older ones arranged themselves in order of seniority. Tekran and Sarba were the youngest. Tekran started to wave Sarba in front of him. Then he checked himself and murmured, 'Maybe not.' He moved ahead of her. He was a year her senior.

Sarba caught up with him, carrying her loaded tray. Her own voice was low too. 'You can't help feeling a bit sorry for Jentiz, can you? To lose both his son and his daughter at one go. It's not just that Balgo's dead; he died in disgrace. And you can tell he adored Alalia.'

Tekran's hands tensed on his tray. 'These roast peppers and stuff look brilliant, don't they? I bet they're fresh out of the market garden here.' He dropped his voice to a whisper. 'Shut up, you fool. You're a Ring-Holder, investigating treason. You can't afford to be sympathetic.'

She opened her mouth to protest that he had pitied Alalia himself, then closed it. She was passing behind Hania's chair. When she set her tray down on an empty table, she was annoyed to find her hands were shaking.

Tekran still stood, looking for a place with the other sorcerers. There were no spare seats. Almost reluctantly, he joined Sarba. His eyes went swiftly to hers, and then dropped. He spoke first.

'Look, Sarba. You're on duty every hour of the day here. Never forget that. I shouldn't even be fraternizing with you like this, in case it looks as if we're getting too friendly, sitting on our own.'

'Their table's full.'

'I know.' He looked sideways at Orzad, who was chatting to Hania. 'But you can be sure that everything we do is being noted. It'll go on your file.'

101

'I haven't done anything to be ashamed of.'

'Make sure you don't.'

'What will happen to Jentiz, if they decide he's guilty of something?'

The young sorcerer bent his head over his plate. The words were so soft she could hardly hear them. 'Depends what. If he was just too soft on Xerappans, they'll strip him of his rank and give him some particularly unpleasant job, down the mines or something. If it's worse, if they think he encouraged Alalia to break the engagement, it could be death. A rather slow and nasty death, to set an example.'

'Death! For that?'

'Defying the High Sorcerer is treason…' His eyes flew up to her face. 'I'm sorry! I thought you knew that. You're his…'

It was difficult for her to speak. 'Lord Cozuman is right, of course. After what happened to my mother.'

'I know. I'm sorry,' he said again. His hand crept out across the table towards hers. Then he caught it back. The two of them continued to eat in silence.

The interrogation dragged on through the long, hot afternoon. Sarba struggled to concentrate.

A picture was building up in her mind. Jentiz had been a decent, loyal officer, an efficient administrator. But there was a side he thought he had kept hidden, a desire to treat his Xerappans with rather more humanity than was normally considered necessary. Was this what made it possible for Alalia to run off with two Xerappans? Sarba knew that this was what Orzad must be thinking.

His wife Emania, it appeared, had not shared his sympathy.

'We were so proud of Balgo. You know he passed his sorcerer's exams with distinction? We had high hopes for him, once he'd served his probationary year here. The High Sorcerer's élite Personal Guard, perhaps, under Digonez.'

'Instead of which,' Orzad said softly, 'Lieutenant Digonez was forced to kill him.'

Jentiz buried his face in his hands.

'Digonez will never marry Alalia now. Would that have pleased you, if the betrothal had fallen through without this drama?'

Jentiz looked up, startled. Sarba tried to read the play of emotions chasing each other across his face. Then his features stiffened.

'It would have been an honour to be united with the High Sorcerer's family.'

'That's not what I asked.'

'Alalia was so excited when she said goodbye to me. She was full of how handsome Digonez was, how he'd picked her out from all the other girls when we visited Mount Femarrat to watch Balgo awarded his sorcerer's rod. She was sure every girl in the colony must be jealous of her. I can't think what happened.'

I can, Sarba thought. I wouldn't want to live with my cousin.

'You haven't answered my question.' Orzad leaned forward. His smile sought to coax the truth from the colonel. 'Would you have been pleased or sorry to see the betrothal broken off, in other circumstances?'

Jentiz sighed. 'One always worries about one's children. I just wanted her to be happy, to have the love of a good man.'

'And did that include Lieutenant Digonez Cozuman?'

'I hardly knew him. He was still a boy in Sorcerer School when I was sent to be governor here.'

'But you know his reputation?'

Jentiz said nothing. Only the veins of his face darkened.

'I see... Ring-Holder Sarba, would you like to ask Colonel Jentiz about his daughter?'

Sarba almost dropped her pencil. Orzad had not

forewarned her. Her mind scrabbled for penetrating, even halfway sensible, questions.

'How did Alalia feel about Xerappans?'

Those two heads close together. One fair, one dark.

'She didn't meet many. I brought her up to be polite to our servants, to treat them fairly. My wife can be... a little impatient with Xerappans. I wanted Alalia to be able to run her own household smoothly. If you treat servants decently, they work better for you.'

'Were Alalia's friends brought up the same way? Or did they feel like your wife?'

'We're in a frontier situation. There are far more Xerappans around us here than in Yadu. It makes some people tense.'

'So what did Alalia think, when you said you couldn't come to her betrothal?'

'Alalia is a sorcerer's daughter.' He was the stiff, disciplined officer again.

'But surely she's human, too. She loved you. She must have wanted you to be there.'

'This was just her betrothal. I'd have hosted her wedding here next year.'

Sarba let her eyes stray to the window. What had Alalia felt, alone in the awesome sanctity of Mount Femarrat, with only her vain, prejudiced mother and her ambitious brother? Without her humane, loving father to strengthen her? Sarba's heart suddenly twisted with the longing to have a father like this herself.

A horn sounded outside. There was a stir of surprise in the room. None of them had noticed how the afternoon sun was declining. Was it time for the Evening Circle already? Questions raced through Sarba's mind. Was she supposed to make the Circle with Vazia and Letti and Hania again on the High Place? Should she leave at once?

Orzad was already getting to his feet, holding out one hand

to Tekran, the other to her. Of course, this colony's Ring-Holders and sorcerers were accustomed to managing without visiting officials. They did not need her. Her place was here.

She moved nearer to the table, to close the circle. She was starting to raise her other hand when the realization hit her. The person closest to her on her right was Jentiz. He, too, was standing, clearly awkward at this sudden change in his situation. Prisoner or not, he must make one of this circle, to call the Power which kept Yadu safe, while Vazia summoned the flame for all of them.

It took another instant for the second realization. Now, and now only, she could hold Jentiz Yekhavu's hand.

She was almost at the edge of the table. It was barely high enough to hide the pouch at her hip. She let her hand drop for a moment, so that the loose sleeve of her robe fell forward. In one swift movement, she scooped up the tiny letter into the palm of her hand. Her fingers curled over it.

What are you doing? The question screamed through her head. *He's under suspicion of treason. You don't know who it's from or what it says.*

Instead of the fragile fold of paper, she seemed to feel against her skin the fluttering of feathers, the beating of the sparrow's heart. The little bird had been terrified, but it had trusted her. It had put its life in her hands to deliver this letter. She had to trust her instinct that Jentiz Yekhavu was a good man.

As she reached out to him, she kept her elbow bent, so that her closed hand was still hidden in her sleeve. He looked sideways in surprise, touching cloth before flesh. Her fist nudged his fingers. Her eyes begged him to betray nothing. Had anyone seen?

Their hands clasped. The letter was caught between them.

They stood in silence. His hand was large, warm over hers. Then the horn sounded again. She must let go. Her own hand was empty.

As the circle broke apart, she took advantage of the general movement to position herself between Orzad and Jentiz just long enough for the colonel to transfer the letter to his pocket. She dared not watch. She did not know if the silent guard on his other side had seen anything.

It had been done in a moment. Colonel Jentiz Yekhavu, Governor of the Mount of Lemon Trees, was on trial for treason. And she had abetted him.

Through the mesh of the window, she caught the bright eye of the sparrow, before it hopped off the ledge and flew away.

Chapter Ten

The garden of the colony's Recreation Centre was abuzz with chatter. Groups gathered round tables under a canopy of vines. The subdued glow of lamps kept back the summer darkness but cast its own distorting shadows. After the glare of the security lights on Mount Femarrat and its walled courtyards, Sarba found the relaxed atmosphere of this colony disconcerting. They have a Fence around them, she told herself, and sentries patrolling. It's quite safe in here. It's only outside, in Xerappan territory, that they're edgy.

'Come and meet my friends.' Letti steered her towards a corner table. High-pitched laughter came from a group of girls gathered round it.

As they approached, into the pool of lamplight, the chatter stilled. The girls turned to stare at Sarba. She was suddenly conscious of being a stranger wearing a Ring-Holder's robe. Letti had changed hers for an ordinary green dress. Sarba had found that somewhat shocking. She had been taught on Mount Femarrat that once you became a Ring-Holder, you were always a Ring-Holder. It was not just a job, but a way of life.

How did Orzad expect these teenagers to accept her as one of them?

'This is Sarba,' Letti introduced her. 'She's staying with us.'

'Hello,' Sarba smiled shyly.

'Come to investigate us, have you?' one of the girls laughed. There was a nervous edge to her voice.

'What's happened to Alalia?'

'Is it true they've arrested the Governor?'

Sarba settled herself on an empty space on a bench. 'Please, I'm off duty,' she lied.

'Nobody here's talking about anything else.'

'They're saying she broke off the betrothal to Digonez. She didn't, did she?'

'After all her airs and graces. It was going to be the betrothal of the century.'

'What are you drinking?' Letti asked.

'Oh, grapefruit juice, please.'

There was a Xerappan at her elbow, pouring juice from a jug beaded with moisture. Sarba felt a shiver of unfamiliarity run down her spine. To be this close to a Xerappan in the half-light felt dangerous. She was not accustomed to the way the colonists used them as servants. Xerappans were not allowed on Mount Femarrat. There had been considerable criticism when the Yekhavus' personal maids and their leopard- and lion-drivers had been let in. After what had happened, it was unlikely ever to occur again.

'Aren't you allowed to tell us anything?' the first girl asked shrewdly.

Sarba nursed the cool beaker between her hands. 'I don't know much. I was on duty at the temple for her betrothal, and, no, she didn't come.'

The girls looked at each other.

'Told you so.'

'She turned him down? The High Sorcerer's nephew?'

'You'd have thought to hear her talk she was over the moon about him.'

'All those lovely dresses she bought for the trip.'

'All the same, when you come to think about it, wouldn't it give you the shivers, marrying into that family? We *need* a tough leader like Lord Cozuman. But would you want him for your uncle?'

Or your father?

'What do you do here?' Sarba asked, to change the subject.

At the end of the table, a girl laughed. 'What do you think? Go to school. Marry a sorcerer. Have sorcerer babies. That's what they want us for, isn't it? We've hardly started here. There's us on the Mount of Lemon Trees and half a dozen other colonies. But when you think of all the rest of Xerappo, waiting for us Yadu to take it over...'

'Need a lot of babies, Chelya. You up for it?'

'Fat chance, when all the decent boys are off at Sorcerer School. I'm just waiting till they come back with their spell-rods.'

There was a riot of laughter.

'Don't girls go away to become sorcerers and Ring-Holders too?'

'A few. We can get jobs here, you know. I work in the nurseries, bringing on new plants. The Xerappans do all the heavy work out in the fields, of course. It's not so bad in the greenhouses. We don't work in the middle of the day.'

'Is that what Alalia wanted to do?'

'Her? I don't know what she wanted – besides Digonez. Do you, Letti?'

'I'd have thought she was more interested in something like teaching, maybe. She was always keen on history, wasn't she?'

'Like she wanted to find out what happened in Xerappo before we came. As if Xerappans had a history!'

Laughter rocked the table, as the silent Xerappan steward cleared away their empty glasses.

'Of course,' said Letti, 'it was beside the point. As Lieutenant Digonez's wife, she wouldn't have needed a job, would she? ... Are you ready, Sarba? It's time for bed, I think.'

Sarba followed her out into the avenue which led to the Ring-Holders' house. A jacaranda tree leaned over the fence and cast a dense patch of shadow. As she passed under it, a hand caught her arm. She gasped. Tekran's voice murmured urgently in her ear.

'Sh! Don't say anything. I just had to tell you… goodbye, Sarba. Please don't think too badly of me tomorrow.'

Astonished, she felt his kiss on her forehead. Then he was gone, loping away into the shadows.

Letti was waiting for her on the path ahead. 'Who was that?'

'Just one of the sorcerers.'

The other girl could not see how her face was burning.

Sarba could not sleep. What could Tekran have meant? *Goodbye, Sarba. Don't think too badly of me tomorrow.*

The strange finality of his words brought her sitting upright. It had sounded terribly as though she would never see him again. What was going to happen tonight?

The room was in darkness. In the opposite bed, Letti was snoring gently. It made it difficult to think. Sarba was not used to sleeping with anyone else.

She threw back the bedclothes and stole barefooted to the window. It was open. She could catch a glimmer of stars between the branches. There was no moon yet.

For a while, she stared into the darkness. Then, as silently as she could, she picked up her sandals and took down her cloak from the peg where she had hung it. Night was colder here. Instinctively, she reached for the glimmer of her bracelet and slipped it on her wrist. She glided back to the window.

Letti stirred. 'Whazzit? … Is that you, Sarba? Is everything all right?'

'Yes. Just going to the bathroom. Go back to sleep.'

Now she would have to go out into the corridor. Could Letti see she was carrying her cloak?

When she came out of the bathroom, she looked at the front door. She did not think there were spells on it. The colonists seemed to trust their Fence. Inside it, they were quite relaxed. But Vazia and Hania's window looked out that way. She had a creepy feeling that she would not get past Hania undetected, even in the Ring-Holder's sleep.

She crept back to Letti's room. The girl's breathing was steady again. She must have rolled over. There were no more snores. Was she really asleep?

She was taking a great risk. If she was caught, she could be sent back to Mount Femarrat in disgrace. It might end her career as a Ring-Holder.

She felt again Tekran's lips on her forehead, his hand on her arm. She had to know.

She dropped her cloak on to the grass below the window, and her sandals after it. She swung a long leg over the sill. Halfway, she paused and looked back. She could not see Letti in the shadows. Would the young Ring-Holder get into trouble for not preventing this?

I was set to spy on Letti. Was she meant to spy on me?

What kind of life was this, when the Children of Yadu couldn't even trust one another?

Her bare feet landed on the warm cloak. She froze for a moment, listening. There was still no sound from Letti. She stole across the garden to the little lane beyond, before she put on her sandals. The cloak was not only warm, it hid her white nightdress. Too late to wish now she had put on her robe. What if she met someone?

Robe or not, if you meet anyone, you'll be in big trouble.

The colonists had planted shade trees along the paths. Sarba avoided the open street and kept to the grass verge, slipping from one tree trunk to another. How lush the well-watered turf was here, when the valley below looked so dry. She made her silent way towards the centre of the colony.

Between the houses, she could see the glimmer of the Fence. The security lights were not as brilliant as those on Mount Femarrat. They were directed outside, illuminating the

111

surrounding hillside. It made the darkness inside the Fence thicker. The street lamps were out.

But there was a light ahead. She recognized the guard post where they had questioned Jentiz.

Suddenly the door burst open, spilling lamplight. Terrified, she shrank back behind the biggest jacaranda tree and crouched down.

A group of uniformed sorcerers came out, talking to each other. Two headed down the road towards her. More fanned out along other streets. Panic seized her. Who were they searching for? Had their spell-rods told them she was out of doors? Or were they already looking for Tekran?

One of the men called over his shoulder to another, 'We'll try that camel of yours against mine next rest day and see who's right.'

'You're on.'

She relaxed a little. Of course, it must be midnight. The sentries were changing over. It was nothing abnormal.

She was just about to get to her feet and move on, when she heard voices coming up behind her. Fool! She had forgotten there would be more sentries coming off duty. She flattened herself against the tree trunk. She counted eight of them, some from the main gate, others from patrolling the perimeter. They disappeared into the guard post. Presently they came out, moving more slowly now, some yawning, and separated homewards.

A single light still glowed inside the building. Was Jentiz Yekhavu sleeping? There must be at least one guard on duty.

What am I doing here? Just because Tekran said something incomprehensible and because I saw a sparrow on the interrogation room window sill? She shivered and pulled her cloak closer around her.

What if Letti has woken up and seen my empty bed?

Her heart raced. There was a movement caught in the

lamplight by the guard-post door. A figure, crouched as she was, crept forward. He drew a spell-rod. The door swung partly open.

As the sorcerer entered, the light fell on his face. Sarba gasped with recognition. *'Tekran!'*

With a desperate glance to check that the road was clear, she raced across it. Tekran whipped round, spell-rod levelled. His hand fell to his side. His face looked appalled.

'Sarba? What on earth are you doing here?' He grabbed her wrist and pulled her inside. 'Shut up and stay there,' he murmured. He closed the door behind them silently.

She felt the intensity of his concentration as he crept towards the room where the light still burned.

A cry of alarm. 'Who's there?'

There was a fizz of spell-light. And words. Sarba covered her ears, stunned. She was losing consciousness, tumbling down a long, dark stair.

She woke to find Tekran bending over her. His face was creased with concern.

'Are you all right? I had to act fast. It was better to make too powerful a spell than one which might not be strong enough to stun the guard.'

'Ouch. My head hurts. It must have been pretty powerful stuff, considering I was standing behind you.'

'I'm not playing games. Why are you here? Were you going to betray me?'

'Betray you? No. Why? What are you doing?'

'Justice, I hope.'

The truth fell clear into place. Tekran letting her go, when he should have reported her for entering the High Sorcerer's house. Tekran's low voice as he remembered how Digonez had terrified Alalia. Tekran telling her what might happen to the governor if he was found guilty.

'Jentiz Yekhavu!' she breathed. It was not even a question.

'Do you think he deserves execution? Because he brought Alalia up not to bully their Xerappan servants? It's not exactly revolution, is it?'

'No. But...'

'Look, Sarba, this is nothing to do with you. Go back now, before it's too late.'

He doesn't know how much it has to do with me. I gave Jentiz the letter.

Aloud she said, 'What were you thinking of doing? There's a Fence. Sentries patrolling all around. You can spell Jentiz's door open, but if you breach the Fence, a whole hornets' nest will break loose on you.'

'Spell-rods can do more than make openings.'

He was moving the rod now, questing. 'This one, I think.'

A smaller sparkle of light this time. As the cell door slowly opened, Jentiz was on his feet facing them. When he saw Tekran's spell-rod, his hand shot instinctively to his own belt, then dropped away. They had taken his rod from him. His face looked grim, resigned.

'So soon?' he said. 'And why the stun-spell a few moments ago?'

'It wasn't meant for you, sir. I had to be sure of overpowering the guard.'

The colonel's eyes widened. 'You're not the death squad? You haven't come to take me to Lord Cozuman?' His glance went past Tekran to Sarba and widened. 'You! You gave me the letter about Alalia!'

Now it was Tekran's turn to look astonished. 'What?'

With an effort, he recollected himself. 'Questions later, sir. We need to get you outside the Fence, fast. I don't think I can manage that, but I think you can.'

He handed Jentiz his spell-rod.

The governor grasped it. His eyes met Tekran's in silent gratitude. 'Hold on to me.'

114

Jentiz and Tekran interlocked hands. Sarba grabbed Tekran's. She heard him gasp. Then his fingers folded over her own and squeezed them tight.

'You're in this deeper than I thought,' he murmured.

Her left hand could not take Jentiz's right, because he was holding the spell-rod. Instead, she grasped his wrist and clung on.

The words were more awful than Tekran's stun-spell. They had the thrilling force of the words the sentries used to open the Fence around Mount Femarrat. Yet this was not the same. No one who was not a sorcerer could ever remember the words of that opening-spell, yet Sarba was sure this was a magic she had never heard before.

She did not have long to think about that, or anything else. Scarcely had Jentiz finished intoning his chant when she felt as though a huge mouth was closing over her, sucking the being from her. She was terrified out of her wits, but she could not scream. She had no breath, she had no body, she was nothing. All around her was... nothing. Not even darkness. She was extinguished, lost.

The mouth spat her out. She was sitting on bare earth. There was a smell of lemons.

Chapter Eleven

In the darkness there were two men talking in low, urgent voices. As Sarba came back to herself, fragments of memory coalesced, along with the atoms of her body. She scrambled to her feet to join Colonel Jentiz and Tekran.

The colonel turned to her apologetically. 'I'm sorry, my dear. I didn't realize you'd never transported before.'

'Don't apologize to her,' said Tekran. 'This is life or death. And it'll still be death if we stay in this orchard.'

Sarba looked behind her, up the hill. Through the dark branches of the lemon trees, she glimpsed the bright perimeter lights of the colony. They were not far away.

'I'm sorry I couldn't get us further from the Fence. It took enough effort, as it was, transporting three of us this far. But we need to be clear of the trees before I bring the camels. Let's move!' Jentiz's voice was swift, decisive. Here was a man accustomed to command. It helped a little to steady the racing fear in Sarba's heart, but not much.

She had broken her vows as a Ring-Holder. She had betrayed her mission. She was outside the Fence.

She followed the others at a run, down through the trees. Starlight lay before her on a bare hillside. She almost didn't see the low wall in front of her. The men vaulted it; she scrambled after them.

They stopped, panting.

'I'm afraid, at this distance, I'll have to bring them one by one.' The spell-rod in Jentiz's hand crackled. 'Carnelian!'

The shadows thickened. There was a terrifying roar. A large camel was kneeling in front of Jentiz.

Light suddenly intensified on the summit. Probing beams swung this way and that.

'They're on to us,' Tekran said grimly. 'That didn't take long.'

'It's not quite that bad. The sentries have sensed something's happened at the Fence, but they don't know what. Not a breach, because the alarms didn't go off. They'll assume someone's trying to break *in*. Xerappan terrorists. We need to be clear of here before they realize it was a break-*out*. Which is your camel?'

'Basalt.'

Again, that crackle of sorcery, the summoning word.

Tekran's camel was kneeling before him.

'And yours? You do have one?'

'Amber.'

She saw the spell-light and heard the name, but even as she was becoming aware of the animal smell, the sense of a large, warm presence nearby, Jentiz gave an exclamation and dropped the suddenly flaming rod.

'That's done it! Counter-magic. Go!' For a moment, he nursed his burned hand. Then he was up and astride Carnelian.

Tekran had snatched up the fallen spell-rod and was mounting Basalt. He glanced over his shoulder. 'You all right, Sarba? Let's hope Amber will follow Basalt…'

They were all staring at the starlit patch of bare earth, where Sarba's mount should have been kneeling. There was nothing there.

Jentiz swore. 'They must have found the sentry in the guard post. They've put up a blocking-spell.'

'Get up behind me. Fast!' ordered Tekran.

She ran to obey. There had been no time for a saddle. She

could feel the spine of the camel below its hump. Before she could settle herself comfortably, Basalt was rising.

At a word from the sorcerers, both camels broke into a run. Sarba clung on to Tekran's waist. Tekran had spoken of camel races, but she had never believed they could move this fast. Stones skidded away from their hooves, bushes flashed past. The night air caught Sarba's cloak and billowed it out behind her. She snatched it back, and wrapped it tight around her, so that it wouldn't slow them down.

'Can you see what's happening behind us?' Tekran called.

She twisted her head. 'It's like a witch-light show! There are coloured flames leaping all over the place. They seem to be scouring the ground outside the Fence.'

'When they find no one there, they'll come after us. *On*, Basalt!'

'I'm slowing you down. He's got to carry two of us.'

'Hold tight! … Wall!' Tekran yelled at Jentiz.

Sarba gasped. A second stone wall stretched across their way, unseen until it was too late to stop. They were not on a path. There was no gate. Could camels jump, like horses?

Simultaneously, both sorcerers spoke a word to their mounts. Tekran held out the spell-rod in front of him.

The camels rose into the air. For a terrifying moment, Sarba felt herself sliding off backwards. She clung on to Tekran, fearing that he would slip, too, on the camel's bare back.

There was a jolt. This time it was the camels who swore. Then they were racing on again, as the land levelled out at the valley bottom.

As they turned on to a road, Tekran looked back. 'Shall I make us invisible?'

'Save your strength,' Jentiz ordered. 'We've got a good start and it's a while yet to dawn. Speed alone may do it.'

They galloped on. It was marginally less frightening on the level track. Sarba looked round again.

'What's *that* coming?'

The sorcerers turned their heads. Caught in the searching witch-beams around the colony, dark shapes were rising. They grew larger as they spread enormous wings. Then they were gathered up into the darkness of the night sky. All that could be seen of them now were the narrow rays of light from their green eyes.

'Dragons!' panted Jentiz. 'That's not something my guards could do. You must have brought some powerful sorcerers with you.'

'We did. Lord Cozuman meant business.'

'And you two young people were part of it? Yet you set me free?'

'We'll talk about that later, if you don't mind, sir. What shall I do?' Tekran had ceased urging Basalt forward. The camels were slowing to a canter.

'Stop. Give me the rod. Then keep very still.'

They reined in their animals. Sarba heard the camels' rasping breath. It was almost harder to keep her balance on the uneven back than when they were galloping. She felt as if the slightest movement would send her slipping off.

This time, Jentiz's spell was only a murmur. He kept the spell-rod protected against his body by his cupped hand. As the light flared briefly, Sarba glimpsed the livid burn on his palm. Then she saw nothing but the faint glimmer of the starlit road. She looked down in alarm. She saw the stones of the track, far below her, and nothing else. She and Basalt and Tekran were invisible. It made her feel strange, almost sick.

She tried to glance up, without breaking her stillness. The green paths of light from the dragons' eyes made a network across the night sky. Then they fanned out from the colony and swept lower, searching the hillsides all around. They probed the lemon orchard, to which Jentiz had transported them, the vegetable fields, the vineyards. They were coming nearer, down the bare lower slopes towards the valley. They lit up the ruined farmhouse, where the family of the Xerappans who had escaped with Alalia had lived. Their eerie light showed dusty fields and stunted crops. They found the road.

With her head half turned, she could see two of them flying along it, scanning either side. It was hard to hold absolutely still, not to scream and flee. She could hardly make out their forms, but the vast space of stars they blotted out told of their size. The rays of their emerald eyes were penetrating. Surely they could see through this guise of invisibility?

'Just keep very still,' Tekran whispered.

The light was on them. She wanted to throw up her arm and shield her eyes. Her fists clenched Tekran's tunic, willing herself not to move.

It was Basalt who moved, flinching from the light and shifting the loose stones of the road.

There was a hiss, like a giant incoming breaker on the shore. A pair of green lights turned towards them. They came homing in.

Jentiz shouted something Sarba could not understand. The spell-light blazed briefly and went out. It took seconds for Sarba to realize that something else had gone out too. Where was the emerald light of the dragon's eyes? Why was the sky overhead suddenly full of stars again?

'He's extinguished it!' Tekran's voice was hushed in awe. 'I could never have done that.'

'Dragons are glamour. A witch-light sending. They're not real.'

'Real enough, in that they're an extension of the mind of the sorcerer who creates them. If it was Orzad, he'll know you snuffed it out.'

'But at least it can't take him back a message of what it saw.'

'*They* can.'

The beams of many more baffled dragons were criss-crossing behind them, frantically searching for their lost comrade. They were focusing on this one spot on the road. The nearest was almost upon them. Jentiz extinguished it, too.

As if at a single command, all the others rose into the air, wheeled, and headed back towards the Mount of Lemon Trees.

Jentiz sighed and suddenly became visible, astride his camel. Sarba could see Tekran, whom she was clinging to, again.

'They know too much. We have to be out of these hills and into the desert by first light. They'll be right on our heels.'

'We're with you.'

The camels broke into a gallop again.

Every bone in her body felt jarred. There was no padded saddle. The track raced past beneath her. Was it only her imagination that the stones shone whiter? Surely it could not be daybreak yet?

Sarba turned her head sideways. A crescent of silver was creeping above the hills. Of course! How could she have forgotten moonrise?

She looked around her. The valley was washed in silver. The track they were following was hardly distinguishable from the stony fields. Hills on either side rose black in shadow. The lights of the Mount of Lemon Trees were dwindling in the distance. But there were lights around Fences on other hills. More colonies ahead. Did the sorcerers have a way of warning them?

'Let me go first,' Jentiz shouted, as the hills closed in and the track took a curve between the two closest.

He disappeared round a shoulder of rock. They did not see what happened. There was a flash of brilliance, more golden than moonlight. Then silence.

Tekran slowed Basalt to a walk.

'I wish I still had my spell-rod,' he muttered. 'I feel helpless, now I've given it to Jentiz. Wait here.'

He slipped to the ground, without bothering to make Basalt kneel. She watched him creep to the rock-slope and peer round. As he stood up and waved to her, she relaxed a little. She kicked her heels experimentally and, to her astonishment, Basalt walked on. Jentiz and Tekran were conferring in the middle of the road.

'A spell-wire,' Jentiz murmured when she drew close. 'Not nearly as powerful as a Fence, but it would have done for us if I hadn't been looking for it. Disabled us, or at least the camels, pretty painfully. The colonies up there have got wind of something. There'll be sorcerers down here any moment.'

'Do we go on?'

'What choice do we have? I'm sorry to have dragged you two into this.'

'As I remember, sir, this was my idea.'

'Oh? I thought it was Sarba's... But we're wasting time.'

Sarba's mind reeled in confusion. Her idea? All she had done was to climb out of the window and go in search of Tekran. How could she have known he was about to free Jentiz?

Something was happening to the thread of sorcerer-light strung across the road, as Jentiz held the spell-rod over it. It split in two, its ends sparking. Two angry snakes of fire twisted upright, straining to reunite. There was barely room for a camel to pass between them. Tekran led Basalt through. Sarba made herself as small as she could on the camel's back, as the flaming snakes hissed on either side of her. Jentiz followed, leading Carnelian. The moment they were past, the snakes leaped for each other. The wire was whole.

'They'll know,' Jentiz said. 'Their sorcerers will have felt it.'

'Is it much further to the desert?' Tekran asked.

'These are the last hills. The sand begins on the other side.'

'What are we going to do when we get to the desert?' Sarba called down. 'Where can we go?'

Jentiz turned to look up at her. The moonlight made unreadable black-and-white crags of his face. There was astonishment in his voice.

'But you were the one who told me.'

There was no time to question what he meant. There was an explosion of flame as a spell-blast slammed into the shoulder of rock behind them, where the road bent into the pass between the hills. The roar of its detonation went on, growing rather than fading. It was not a spell now. An avalanche of stones and earth was hurtling down. The panicked camels took off. Sarba clung on to Basalt's hump for dear life.

Tekran, on the ground, had flung his arms round the black camel's neck. He was being dragged along the road at high speed. Somehow he managed to swing his body up and over. He was not sitting where he should be, high on the camel's back, but lying flat, almost on Basalt's neck. Jentiz had managed to vault on to Carnelian, and work his seat somewhat higher. Daring to let go of Basalt, Sarba leaned forward and hauled Tekran towards her.

'That was Cozuman's sorcerers, not the colonies',' yelled Jentiz. 'They're still to come.'

Jentiz and Tekran were both looking up the hillsides, one on either side. Sarba remembered how their summits had looked from the Mount of Lemon Trees, each one flattened to build a town of white houses for the Yadu. They would be full of sorcerers, under orders now to stop the traitors at all costs.

She was a traitor. She was under sentence of death.

The gap between the hills was so narrow, she could not see the towns above, only the almost vertical cliffs. Lights flashed across the narrow strip of sky. The sorcerers up there could not see them, either.

But the spells had their effect. Ahead of them now, more boulders came tumbling down, bouncing and crashing on to the road. Basalt swerved, almost flinging Sarba and Tekran off. The young sorcerer was leaning forward, keeping up a stream of soft, urgent encouragement to his mount. She felt ashamed to think that she had once joked with him about camel racing. Just behind them, Jentiz and Carnelian were steering their own dangerous course. These were deliberate missiles, not an unintended avalanche.

Sarba leaned forward and shouted in Tekran's ear, 'Why aren't the Mount Femarrat sorcerers still firing spells from behind us?'

He did not answer. A boulder as big as a house thundered in front of them, cracking in two. For a moment it seemed that Basalt must crash into it, or catapult them from his back as he skidded to a stop. But with a twist of his sinewy body he swerved aside and raced for the narrow gap between boulder and cliff. They were round it, and the moonlit sky was opening out in front of them.

'They didn't mean to set off that avalanche at the bend back there,' Tekran panted at last. 'It didn't hit us, but I guess it's stopped *them*. For the moment.'

Jentiz was alongside them now, looking upwards. Sarba saw more streaks of green cut across the stars.

'Dragons again!'

Tekran shot a look at the colonel. 'Sir, can you do it again? If you're tiring...' He reached out a hand, as if he would take the spell-rod.

'I'm all right.' Jentiz looked exhausted. His sweat glistened in the moonlight. 'Just a little bit further...'

Suddenly the level road ended. As the cliffs fell behind them, the track split in two, winding up the less vertical slopes. Before and below them stretched a silver sea. The camels' hooves sank into sand.

'The desert?' cried Tekran.

'From here on.'

Jentiz raised the spell-rod with an effort. His arm shook as he held it out. As he spoke the words of power, he was looking at the sky.

The moonlight dimmed. A breeze whipped Sarba's hair sideways across her face. There was a stinging on her skin.

'Cover yourselves,' Jentiz shouted.

The men wrapped their faces in the scarves which hung from the back of their caps. Sarba drew her cloak over her head. Sand assaulted them. It seemed to be coming from every side. Where it found exposed skin, it was like grazing herself on rough rock. It was in her hair, on her lips. She buried her face against Tekran, and knew that he had no such protection in front of him.

Still, miraculously, the camels went on. They were plodding now, not racing. Sometimes the wind swept their groans back to her, but mostly it was the howl of the wind itself she heard.

Their progress seemed unbearably slow. Gradually she became aware that the darkness of the storm was not total, that the sand lodged on Tekran's uniform was gold, not silver, that his tunic was red. Day had come.

Somewhere beyond the whirling sand, the sun was about to rise. With the instinct of years of training, one thought rose uppermost in Sarba's mind. It was time for the Morning Circle. She gave a little hiccup of near-hysterical laughter. Three days ago, she had been a Ring-Holder on Mount Femarrat. She had climbed to the temple in her clean white-and-red robe, held hands with the others, performed the chants which brought down the Power to the copper bowl on the jasper Stone. What was she now? A disgraced fugitive, in a nightgown filthy with sand, and an anonymous cloak, with no home, no refuge, lost in the untracked desert. Only her bracelet told of her past.

She thought of asking Jentiz and Tekran to form a Circle, remembering how the party from Mount Femarrat had done that on camel-back. But she could barely see Jentiz, and he was straining every nerve to keep the storm-spell going. Somewhere behind them, other powerful sorcerers would be battling to break it. And they were so far out now that even the Mount of Lemon Trees seemed remote and unreal. Could the Power reach this far? Could it keep them safe here?

She made a circle of her arms round Tekran, and hummed the chants to herself.

Suddenly, she was pitched forward. She could not see the ground under Basalt's hooves clearly, but they must have topped a ridge. They were plunging steeply down. She felt the soft, blown sand dragging at the camel's legs. They were hardly moving.

Yet the day was lightening. The sand blowing past her was thinning. She could see Jentiz clearly. He could barely hold the rod up. She could only see his eyes between his cap and his scarf. They were dark with exhaustion.

'Sir, do you want me to take over? If we've lost the other sorcerers, I should be able to manage a spell-wind by myself. As long as I don't have to fight their counter-spells.'

Jentiz loosened his scarf and gave a tired smile. 'You can try, lad. But I think it's time to take cover.'

He dropped from his camel and spoke softly to it. Carnelian knelt. Tekran brought Basalt to his knees and helped Sarba down. The camels lowered their weary heads.

'Give me your cloak, Sarba.'

Tekran was already busy, scooping a hollow in the side of the sand dune. When she saw what he was doing, Sarba went to help him, unfastening her cloak and passing it to Jentiz.

They sat huddled in the lee of the ridge, with Sarba's cloak spread over them. Tekran did his best with the spell-rod, but the wind was dying. Sand still fell over them, turning the dark

126

wool of the cloak to yellow, but it was petering out. Blue sky was showing. Tekran spoke the words louder this time, looking anxiously at the white rod.

Jentiz caught his wrist. 'It's not you, lad. I was finding it more and more difficult. I know I'm tired, but it's more than that.'

'So I'm not imagining it?' Tekran said quietly. 'There isn't the power in the rod that there should be.'

'We're a long way from home. When we set up our colony on the far side of the border, the Power of Mount Femarrat didn't seem to reach us as strongly as it should. That's why we made our own small High Places, with their own Stones.'

'Then, sorcery won't work out here?'

'I think it may not, or only weakly.'

'Hania has a portable Stone and copper bowl. I should have brought them.' Sarba gave a little laugh, to hide her fear. 'To think, I carried that heavy flask of oil for nothing.'

'There's one advantage,' said Jentiz grimly. 'The Sorcerer Guard may have difficulty flying dragons over the desert to search for us.'

'All the same,' Tekran said, 'I'm glad we're under cover now it's daylight.'

They felt the weight of the drifted sand on the folds of the cloak above them. Even black Basalt and the reddish gold of Carnelian were almost smothered. From the air, they would be indistinguishable from the surrounding desert.

'Something else I would have brought if I'd known: food and water,' Sarba tried to smile.

Tekran unhooked a flask from his belt and passed it to her. She unscrewed the cap.

'Water!'

'Standard equipment. But that's all there is.'

She took a mouthful and passed it to Jentiz. It was hardly enough to wash the sand from her lips.

'Can you magic food? I mean, could you, if the Power was strong enough?'

'We could. But it wouldn't nourish you.'

'The sandstorm was real enough.'

'If those sorcerers from Mount Femarrat had got nearer, it wouldn't have been. They tried to break our spell.'

'The sorcerer-wind did its work,' Jentiz said. 'And the sand itself is real.'

They sat in silence for a while.

Then Sarba said, 'What are we going to do? We can't go back, even if we knew where *back* is. We're out in the desert. Ahead of us there's just... nothing.'

Jentiz's head shot up, dislodging a shower of sand. '*You* say that?'

'Why shouldn't I? It's true, isn't it?'

'But the message...?'

'What message?'

'This.'

Her heart contracted suddenly, as the colonel drew from the pocket of his tunic a tiny, folded piece of yellow paper.

'Didn't you know what was in it?'

She shook her head.

'Yet you risked your life to give it to me?'

'What's all this about?' Tekran asked, looking from one to the other. But Sarba's eyes held Jentiz's steadily.

'A sparrow brought it to me. It was tied to its leg with ribbon. I could feel how terrified it was, but it let me catch it and untie the letter. Someone knew I was going to meet you, even before I knew it myself. The letter had your name on it. The sparrow trusted me. And when I met you, I trusted you.'

'I should say thank you, but it doesn't seem enough.'

'It was Tekran who got you out of the guard post. That was nothing to do with me.'

'I owe my life to both of you.'

128

'We may not have much life left. We've only got this one flask of water.'

He passed her the letter. The wax seal was broken.

She unfolded the little square of paper and read, *'You will find Alalia at the Forgotten City. Follow the Mermaid.* Alalia! Your daughter?'

'She must be alive! And she's safe, where I hope the Sorcerer Guard can never catch her.'

'But why would someone give this to me? I've only seen Alalia once, and even then, I never spoke to her.'

'And what does it mean? I've never heard of a Forgotten City,' said Tekran.

'Alalia was curious about the history of Xerappo, before we colonized it. So I asked the local schoolteacher and passed on to her everything he told me. She was particularly fascinated by stories of oases in the desert, of lost cities. They say some were once fabulously wealthy, trading places for caravans from all over the world, bringing treasures to Xerappo. It's wonderful to think that Alalia may have found one of them. That she could be there now, waiting for me. '

'But the Xerappans seem so poor and helpless. They don't have sorcery, or anything.'

'They're poor now. They haven't always been.'

'That still doesn't explain. Why send the letter to *me*?'

'Maybe you should ask your sparrow.'

The sun was climbing higher, the sky taking on a brilliant blue. For a little while, their cave of sand had preserved the coolness of the night, but the heat was growing.

Jentiz took back the letter and fondled it. 'I couldn't bear the thought that I didn't know what had happened to her, or if she was still alive. You've no idea what it meant to me, reading this.'

'Why didn't whoever wrote this letter send the sparrow straight to the Mount of Lemon Trees?' Sarba wrinkled her forehead, thinking hard. 'How did they know that you'd be in a cell with bars and wire mesh over the window? What told them that I was the person who could, and would, deliver it to you? I wouldn't even have believed it myself.'

There was a silence. The sleeping camels breathed heavily, under their burrows of sand.

'Maybe this Forgotten City has a wisdom we have lost.'

'You think we can find it?' asked Tekran. 'Out there in the desert?'

'*Follow the Mermaid*. That's what the letter says.'

'We must be a hundred miles from the sea.'

'But we're under the stars.'

They followed Sarba's gaze up to the cloudless blue sky.

'Of course!' Jentiz said softly. 'The Mermaid constellation.'

Chapter Twelve

They slept. They had agreed to keep watch, turn and turn about. Jentiz was clearly at the end of his strength. All night, he had battled with sorcerers as powerful as himself, and many more in number. Tekran, too, had used spells beyond the norm for his rank, and for the first time in deadly earnest. They were all worn down by terror, by magic, by the headlong gallop on bareback camels, by heat and hunger and thirst.

'I'll take the first watch,' Sarba insisted. 'I haven't done as much as you two have.'

She sat, shrouded in her cloak, bearing the weight of sand on her shoulders. The two sorcerers lay stretched out beside her, instantly asleep. Did she only imagine that the lines of grief carved in Jentiz's face had softened? At least he knew now that Alalia was still alive. When she turned her gaze to Tekran, her heart turned over. Those ridiculous tufts of his eyebrows. The fuzz of golden down on his chin, where he needed a shave. Can I do anything to protect them? she wondered. I'm a Ring-Holder, aren't I?

But was she? She had broken her vows. She stared down at the orange-red bracelet on her arm. She had worn it for more than a year, yet it seemed to belong to a stranger.

With just this bracelet, without her robe, without Stone, without flame, could she still be a Ring-Holder? Could she call down the Power to keep them safe? What was this Power? It was not a question anyone on Mount Femarrat had dared to ask. It just *was*. The Power was what they served. It was the

131

reason for everything they did, and the strength in which they did it. The Power commanded obedience, and her father was its voice.

She had disobeyed. She must have broken at least a hundred rules. She had defied the very sorcerers her father had sent to root out treason. She was a traitor herself.

They would cast her out. They would speak spells and curses against her. They would tear her name out of the Book of Ring-Holders.

What does it matter? I'm going to die, anyway. Lost in the desert without food and water.

You're only feeling low because you're hungry and thirsty and tired. Once you've had a good meal and a sleep, things won't seem so bad.

A meal? Here?

She waited as long as she could, hunched and miserable. Her head was heavy and hot.

Basalt coughed. Sarba started awake, dislodging a shower of sand. Her head had fallen on to her bent knees.

The shadows of the camels' humps had shifted. The sun was moving towards noon. Reluctantly, she shook Tekran, trying not to disturb the still-sleeping Jentiz.

There was a moment when he stretched and opened his eyes, as if in his own bed in the sorcerers' hostel. He saw her looking down at him and his forehead creased, puzzled. Then she saw in his eyes the sudden flood of knowledge. He was instantly wide awake, sitting up. His taller body lifted the weight of the sand-filled cloak from her. He smiled at her, and suddenly the world seemed brighter.

'I feel loads better for that. How long have I slept?'

'From the shadows, I guess it's about midday.'

'Have you had anything to drink?'

'No. There's so little left.'

'You're a noble lot, you Ring-Holders. Some of the

132

sorcerers I know would have swigged the whole flask while Jentiz and I were sleeping. You need some, though, to keep going. Have a mouthful.'

It was an exquisite torture, to drink just one mouthful and no more. Tekran did the same. He shook the flask. There was the lightest swish.

'We'll save the rest for Jentiz.'

'What will we do when it's gone?'

'Hope? We can't stay here, that's for certain.'

'Can we find this Forgotten City before we die?'

'If Alalia can do it, it has to be possible.'

Her stomach growled with hunger. They both laughed.

'Sleep,' ordered Tekran. 'Forget it for a few hours. My watch.'

But when she woke in the late afternoon, Tekran was asleep again, with his head on his knees, and Jentiz was awake.

'We have to move,' Jentiz said, 'as soon as night falls. We're rested now, but without food or water, we'll be getting weaker by the hour. We've no idea how far it is to the Forgotten City. It could be several days' journey.'

Tekran and Sarba looked at each other in undisguised dismay.

'I never thought I'd wish I was a camel,' Tekran said. 'But right now, having a hump to store provisions would come in handy.'

'The sparrow must have flown with the letter from the Forgotten City to Mount Femarrat. It can't be that far, can it?'

'Birds can fly thousands of miles.'

'Alalia had been missing less than two days when I got the letter.'

The men stared at her. Jentiz struck his thigh.

'You're right! There has to be hope. If only we can find it.'

'I wish I'd paid more attention to Navigation in Sorcerer School,' Tekran said. 'Travelling by night, we could pass within a couple of miles and never see it. Sorry! I shouldn't have said that, should I?'

'It's true, though, isn't it?' said Sarba quietly.

The westering sun turned the ridge of dunes to ruddy gold. As if they sensed the time was near, the camels snorted and shook the piled sand from their backs. As she watched the sunset, Sarba turned diffidently to the others.

'It's time for the Evening Circle.'

In silence, the sorcerers held out their hands. The three of them joined.

Sarba was suddenly unsure what to do. Only the duty Ring-Holders and sorcerers in the temple made the ceremony to bring down the fire. Everywhere else, people just held hands in silence. Were they too far out, even from the Mount of Lemon Trees, for that?

Softly, she began to hum. She wondered if Tekran might draw his spell-rod and try to call the flame, even though there was no Stone or copper bowl. He stood unmoving, with his head bowed. Her lips parted and the chant was flowing from her now. Her voice felt rough in her dry mouth. Was it ridiculous? Would it have the opposite effect? Was the Power angry with her?

The sand flared in the last rays of the setting sun. Just for a mad moment, she thought it was a flame. Then the light died. The shadow of night fell over the desert.

Jentiz dropped her hand and looked up at the sky. 'The stars are coming out.'

They watched intently as the first faint pricks of light showed through the fading sky. As the darkness deepened, patterns emerged. They scanned the western horizon, their imaginations joining star to star with invisible lines.

That night was like none Sarba had ever known. She had

not realized the sky could be so enormous, so black, so deep. All her life, she had been protected by the harsh glare of security lights around Mount Femarrat. Now she felt this darkness could swallow her, could swallow the whole earth, and leave only the tiniest pinprick of starlight. That must be what these stars were: other earths, other suns. She had known that in her head. She had never felt it before. It was not the stars that amazed her, brilliant though many of them were; it was the enormity of the darkness which surrounded them.

She watched, awed, while Jentiz and Tekran scanned the horizon, tracing out the pattern of constellations.

'The Vine, the Hunter, the Cobra... Where *is* it?'

'There? Isn't that smudge of little stars the fall of her hair?'

Sarba followed Tekran's pointing arm to the south-west. At first, she saw only a random scatter of stars, some brilliant, others small and pale. Gradually, her mind composed them into a recognizable shape. Hair which flowed in a haze of a thousand tiny stars, outspread arms, a curving fishtail.

'There? That's where we have to go?' She swallowed a lump in her throat. *There* was far out in the desert, in the opposite direction from the Mount of Lemon Trees and the other colonies, from the border Fence, from the land of Yadu and Mount Femarrat. That way led out over the horizon, across a wilderness of sand.

'It's a huge risk,' said Tekran quietly. 'We've no food and only a mouthful of water left. Out there, there's... nothing. We'll probably die.'

'We'll die if we go back to the sorcerers,' said Jentiz. 'And we'll die if we stay here. I'll settle for "probably".'

Tekran rose, without saying anything more. He called to Basalt. In equal silence, Jentiz readied Carnelian. Sarba picked up her cloak, which had sheltered them from sandstorm and sun. She shook it free of the weight of clogging sand and slipped it over the stained white nightgown. The night was growing rapidly colder.

'We should waste no time.' Jentiz was mounted and his camel was rising. In another moment, Basalt bore Tekran and Sabra aloft.

'There's one problem with following the Mermaid,' Jentiz said drily. 'Stars rise and set. As the night goes on, I fancy our Mermaid may slip beneath the horizon.'

'Time to ride then,' said Tekran.

The long rest had not made the camels any better-tempered. They groaned and hissed alarmingly as their riders coaxed them into motion. The travellers turned their faces towards the Mermaid and committed themselves to the desert.

Sarba looked back at their fragile shelter in the side of the dune. Their sand cave had already collapsed.

'The storm covered our tracks from the colonies, but won't we make new ones tonight?'

'We're a long way out. Further than sorcerers have been yet. Colonel Gordoz doesn't even know which direction we took. If they search for us on camels, it could be a long time before they pick up our traces.'

'And if they use dragons?'

'They could see us, even by night, but they'd have to be lucky. This desert's a very big place. And that's if dragon magic can hold this far.'

Tekran drew his spell-rod. As they rode forward, he looked down at it in his hand and gave a strange, twisted smile. 'Five years I studied to earn this. My mum and dad were so proud of me. Their little boy, one of the Sorcerer Guard on Mount Femarrat. Now you're telling me this is going to be useless here? Sorcery won't work?'

'I didn't say spells wouldn't work at all. But you know what we felt last night. No matter how hard we tried, the magic was fading.'

Tekran's face was almost comical in its dismay. 'Then what am I for? I'm a sorcerer. What else am I good for?'

'I know.' The older man's voice was more sober. 'It's been my whole life. Using the Power to conquer Yadu, to take over Xerappo, to guard the colony. I feel naked without it. I haven't even *got* my spell-rod.'

'You can borrow mine, sir, any time.'

'But, as you say, what use is it here? What use am I?'

Or me, thought Sarba. What use is a Ring-Holder with no flame?

'It feels better to be doing something positive,' Tekran said after a while. 'Not just running away, but travelling towards something. It's a good job they taught us to ride camels bareback at Sorcerer School.'

'You were pretty good last night,' Sarba said. 'A flat-out gallop, with no reins.'

She did not remember seeing Tekran blush so deeply before.

'Basalt and I understand each other quite well. Though a little magic helped.'

After the panic of their flight the night before, it seemed almost restful to be pacing across the starlit sand alone. The desert was not the uniform sea of sand Sarba had imagined. It had hills and valleys, ridges of hard-packed crystals and troughs where the camels' hooves sank deep.

Long after they were weary and punished by thirst, Jentiz slowed his mount beside theirs. 'Look, the moon's just coming up over the horizon. By my reckoning, the night should be half over. Time for the last of the water. There are just a few drops left.'

Tekran gave Sarba the flask first. It was a terrible responsibility. She longed for a deep, life-saving gulp, but there were still the other two. How little water was there? She took a few sips, letting it wet her parched lips and tongue. Had she been too self-sacrificing? Was her share really greater? She pushed the thought away and handed the flask back to Tekran. There was no way of knowing how little was left when it came to Jentiz.

Tekran stowed the empty flask in his saddlebag. Their silence told of the huge question in front of them. When might they next find water? Would they reach it in time?

The constellation of the Mermaid still hung clear of the horizon. The spangled tail glittered with scales of blue and green. It had never occurred to Sarba before that stars had colours.

'We mustn't be fooled. When she swims out of sight, we must steer by the constellation above her. If that letter's right.'

Sarba was almost asleep, with the swaying gait of the camel and the warmth of Tekran's body in front of her, inviting her to lay her head against him and rest. Suddenly, she was aware of a change in the motion. Basalt was quickening his pace. Tekran had jerked upright, nearly dislodging her from her perch behind him.

The moonlight was brilliant.

'What's *that*?' His voice was hoarse with thirst and disbelief.

'Trees? It must be an oasis!'

'The camels certainly think so. I can hardly rein Basalt back.'

'Bless you, little sparrow, bless you!'

'It's just in time. The stars are fading. It'll be morning soon.'

'Do you think the Sorcerer Guard could pursue us, even out here?' Sarba asked. 'Without magic?'

'Don't write the sorcery off too soon. It's weaker, certainly, so far from Mount Femarrat and the colonies' sanctuaries. But I wouldn't like to swear it's quite dead.'

Jentiz said, 'Much would depend on the strength of the sorcerer who tried to use it. Magic takes an effort of will.'

'You could still use my spell-rod?' Tekran asked. 'If you had to?'

'Perhaps.'

Sarba could see them clearly now against the paling sky. The feathery mops of palm trees, clustered around... She must not let herself dream of a pool of water. What if this were just a mirage, a trick of the twilight, an illusion from hoping too much?

It was the smell which told her it was real. She had never noticed before the rich scent of vegetation, of trees, even when they were not laden with fragrant blossom. Now she could see the heavy clusters of dates drooping from their branches.

'Food, as well as water?'

They were all jumping to the ground, almost before their camels had knelt. It was hard not to run towards the trees. Only long discipline as sorcerers and Ring-Holder kept them to some semblance of self-control.

'It must be here,' said Jentiz urgently. 'In the middle of the trees.'

Tekran was kneeling. 'There's no pool... but the sand is damp.'

Frantically he was digging with his hands, like a dog with its paws. Sarba knelt to help. Damp sand became wet. Moisture was cold on her fingers. She lifted them to her mouth and sucked, regardless of the clinging sand.

Down they went, until there was an undeniable pool around their hands. They drank thirstily, bathed their faces, rinsed off the sand. At last they were satisfied. Tekran filled his flask. They made way for the camels to reach down their long necks and slurp what they could.

'Dates,' Jentiz said, standing up and looking above their heads. 'How's your head for heights, Tekran?'

Tekran shook the tree. Nothing happened. He eyed the

ridges of the trunk, where the leaf sprays of past years had fallen away. 'Not much of a foothold.'

'If I stood on your shoulders,' suggested Sarba, 'I might be tall enough.'

She balanced shakily, glad of the tree trunk to hold on to. Tekran wavered upright, supporting her.

'Of course, I could have suggested you stood on Basalt. He's taller than I am.'

'No, thank you very much. This is bad enough. I think I can reach.'

She grasped the nearest bunch of dates and pulled. It was harder than she had hoped. The cluster refused to come away in her hand. And she was not quite tall enough to pick the individual dates.

'Do you have a knife?' she called down to Jentiz.

'They took it, along with my spell-rod, when they arrested me.'

'There's one on my belt,' Tekran said. 'Can you unclip it and pass it up to her?'

There was an unsettling change in Tekran's position, then Jentiz was holding the knife as high as he could. It was scary to let go and lean down just a little to take it.

It was in her hand. She sawed through the stem and the date cluster tumbled to the ground. She licked the stickiness from her fingers.

'Can you reach any more, while you're at it?'

She harvested three more clusters, before her arms refused to stretch any further.

'Can I come down now?'

Her experience of a camel made it seem not quite so unfamiliar as Tekran bent his knees and lowered her to the ground.

'They may be dates, but are they ripe?'

'I could eat palm leaves, I'm so hungry.'

The dates were just coming to ripeness, still rather hard, but yielding a satisfying sweetness. They shared one bunch and stowed away the rest.

'We've another day of life in front of us.' Tekran's face was serious with gratitude.

'Food for more, but only one flask to carry water,' Jentiz reminded him.

'How many days travelling did Alalia say it was?'

'She didn't,' put in Sarba.

Jentiz scanned the paling sky. 'The sun will be up soon. At least we have shade here. We should sleep while we can, then another night's riding. I'll keep the first watch.'

'Are you still worried about sorcerers?' Sarba asked.

'I'm always worried about the Sorcerer Guard.'

'But you were one of them.'

'That's why.'

It seemed like luxury, to be stretched out under the shade of palm trees, with a waterhole near at hand if she got thirsty, and dates hanging overhead. Sarba raised her sleepy head on her crooked arm and eyed the burning sands through the tree trunks. Surely, no one could track them out here? Their route from the colonies had been lost in the sandstorm. The power of sorcery was too faint here to sustain the searching dragons in the sky. How could anyone find them?

She thought it was her tired eyes which made the scene shift. She blinked and focused again. Still the illusion that something was moving across the sands. She stared harder. It was coming nearer. Fear gripped her stomach. It was not her imagination. Someone was riding towards the oasis.

Chapter Thirteen

A lone figure on a camel. She registered that much before she shook Tekran violently awake. 'Someone's coming!'

She knew from the tension in Jentiz's tall figure that he had already seen. The younger sorcerer was alert instantly, his spell-rod out.

'Put it away,' Jentiz said quietly. 'If we can manage this without sorcery, so much the better.'

'I'm sorry. I can't change what I am so easily, can I?'

'It may be a perfectly innocent traveller.'

'And it may not.'

Sarba's nerves were screaming for them to mount the camels and race away. To put the screening oasis between them and this stranger approaching.

It would not work. There were still hours to sunset. If this man was really pursuing them, he would see and follow.

'At least we're in the shelter of the trees. We'll have the advantage of surprise.'

The stranger came on. They could see him distinctly now. He wore a loose, flowing robe of brown. Round his head was wound a yellow scarf, which hid everything except his eyes. There was nothing surprising about this. It was the way Xerappans traditionally dressed in desert country. Yet it made Sarba shiver with a different sort of fear.

'He's a Xerappan.'

'Or wearing Xerappan clothes.'

Jentiz was wary, as she was.

The man was riding an unremarkable sandy-brown camel.

They could not be sure of the moment he became aware of them in the shadows of the palms. He continued to ride forward without a check. Almost, Sarba thought with a shudder, as though he expected to see them here. Through a slit in the enveloping yellow scarf, they saw his eyes staring at them. Dark eyes, Xerappan eyes. Yet these did not have the cringing fear and subservience of the eyes of the conquered people who had remained in the land of Yadu.

Sarba did not want to be this close to him.

The stranger swung down from his camel. He stood tall for a Xerappan. He gave a bow which had as much of hostility in it as courteous greeting.

'Peace be with you.'

'And with you.'

His eyes travelled over the men's red uniforms. 'It's not often we see Yadu sorcerers this far out in the desert. What is your business here?'

Jentiz and Tekran exchanged glances. They were clearly calculating how much it was safe to tell him.

Jentiz made a bold move. 'To tell you the truth, we're in trouble with our own people. We're on the run.'

'And where are you running to?'

'To wherever we can find water and food and a safe haven.'

He had trusted the Xerappan so far, to gain his sympathy, but the colonel was not going to reveal their destination and Alalia's refuge.

'It's a bold man who sets off across the desert, not knowing where the next oasis is.'

'Desperation can make any of us bold. The Sorcerer Guard are after us.'

The dark eyes flickered. 'Do you think they could follow you here?'

'I hope not. The further they get from Mount Femarrat, and

143

from the lesser sanctuaries in the colonies, the weaker the power of their sorcery becomes. They couldn't sustain the flying dragons they sent after us.'

'And your power of sorcery, too, must weaken.'

'Exactly.'

Listening, Sarba found this disturbing. She had never met a Xerappan who seemed so unafraid of the Yadu, even of Yadu sorcerers. There was a grim pride about this man, as though he owned this land. As, I suppose, Sarba thought, he does. We are the strangers here; he is at home.

'Where are you going yourself?' she asked. 'This oasis must be on the road to somewhere, for you to stop here.'

He turned to her, as if surprised to find she had a voice. Is it not usual for Xerappan women to question men? she wondered. She didn't know.

'My way is my own,' he said. The answer annoyed her. Hadn't he asked the same question of them? 'Like you, I sought a place to rest in the heat of the day, and water my camel.'

Sarba reached out a hand to his stolid, sandy beast. Not a distinctive black racing camel, like Basalt, nor like the colonel's lean, highly trained mount. Just an ordinary sand-coloured camel. It turned its steady eyes to her, fringed with curling lashes. They were just like Amber's eyes. She felt a pang of nostalgia now for the steady animal which had carried her safely from Mount Femarrat to the Mount of Lemon Trees, when she had never ridden a camel before. Her hand caressed the hairy neck.

'Careful,' warned Tekran. 'They bite.'

But the sandy camel stood placidly under her stroking.

'If you don't mind,' said his rider, 'I need to eat and rest.'

He led the beast to the pool. The animal pawed the wet sand, enlarging the hole the Yadu had made. It splayed its legs, lowered its head and drank deeply and noisily. It seemed to go on for a long time. Only when the animal had finished did the Xerappan kneel to drink himself. He slipped the yellow scarf from his mouth. A short, curling beard hid his lower face.

When he was satisfied, he filled a flask, like the one Tekran carried. He opened his saddlebag and drew out a loaf of bread. When he saw them watching him, he broke off a hunk and held it out. His teeth smiled.

'Please, share my food.'

They thanked him politely, trying to disguise their eagerness.

'I used to like dates,' said Tekran. 'Funny how you can go off things.'

The unleavened bread was drying in the desert heat, but it made a welcome contrast to the sticky dates. The four of them sat in the shade, eating, while the pitiless sun strengthened over the sands.

'My name is Jentiz, Colonel Jentiz,' said Alalia's father, as though the gift of food merited a confidence in return. 'And this is Sorcerer Tekran and Ring-Holder Sarba.'

She noticed that he did not add her surname, Cozuman. She knew the shudder that name would have sent through any Xerappan. It might well have shortened her life.

Yet the stranger was looking at her with sudden intensity. 'A Ring-Holder? Of course, she wears her bracelet.'

Sarba looked down. She had almost forgotten the band of carnelian which encircled her wrist. On Mount Femarrat, it had been a ritual act to put it on each morning with her white-and-red robe. Was it habit that had made her do it, even in the middle of the night on the Mount of Lemon Trees? They had put so many miles between her and the ceremonies of the Ring-Holders that she had lost the sense of its significance. She realized guiltily that she had slept through some of those ceremonial hours. This bracelet had once been her mark of

145

office, as important to her as the spell-rod to a sorcerer. This was how she had called down the Power to light the flame.

What would a Xerappan know about that? Why should he care?

She twisted the bracelet thoughtfully. Did she only imagine she felt a faint pulse of power? Even out here?

She became aware that Jentiz was waiting. He was staring at the stranger, politely, but as if he was expecting something from him. At last he said, quite quietly, 'We have trusted you with our names. Will you not tell us yours?'

Something flickered in the man's dark eyes. There was a fractional hesitation. 'Barak,' he said.

They all knew it was not the truth.

They separated to sleep, the three Yadu close to the well, Barak some distance away. As the sandy camel passed Basalt and Carnelian, he stopped four-square with the obstinacy of his breed. He gave a whicker, as though of greeting. Basalt reached out his long black neck towards the newcomer.

'That's odd,' said Tekran. 'They usually swear at a strange camel.'

The Xerappan spoke sharply. This time his camel did swear, softly. But he followed his master among the trees. The others watched from a distance, as the man ordered the animal to kneel, and then lay down himself beneath the palms. The size of the oasis meant that he was barely in sight.

'Not very sociable, is he?' said Tekran.

'Would you be, if you were a Xerappan, and you met a bunch of Yadu sorcerers in what you thought was free Xerappan territory?'

A shaft of understanding lit Sarba's mind. Jentiz really does care about Xerappans. He's a colonel of the Sorcerer Guard, yet he can imagine what it feels like to be one of the conquered people. That's where Alalia Yekhavu gets it from. That's why she fled with her Xerappan driver and her maid.

146

And this, the voice of conscience told her, is what Examiner Orzad wanted you to discover. This is the evidence which could damn him, the proof of his disloyalty to Yadu.

This is what your father has spent his life on Mount Femarrat protecting us all from.

She had thrown away her future as a Ring-Holder to save this man.

Yet it was a step too far for herself. She could sympathize with Jentiz, but never with the Xerappans.

It was a relief to be able to speak plainly. 'Do you trust him?' she asked Jentiz. 'Can we trust any Xerappan, considering who we are?'

'If we find the Forgotten City, we shall have to.' The father's voice was steady, but it was a rebuke. 'It must have been Xerappans who saved Alalia's life when she fled Mount Femarrat. The only future she has now is with them. And it must be our future too.'

Sarba's skin crawled. She had known it, of course. It was obvious. But she had never until now allowed herself to think what it would mean. To live forever surrounded by those dark-haired, dark-eyed people, who would remind her daily of the ones who had poisoned her mother.

Confused, she went back to the space in the shade and lay down to rest, leaving Jentiz to resume his watch. She scooped out a hollow for her hip and drew her cloak across her. The sun was barely an hour above the horizon. Soon it would be too hot to need any covering. But now it made a welcome darkness over her eyes.

She peeped through the gap she had left to breathe. She could see their two camels under the trees nearby. They were kneeling, at rest. Carnelian's jaws moved with a circular motion, chewing on the leaves and stalks of a date cluster. Basalt seemed to be gazing beyond them, to where, on the far side of the oasis, the Xerappan lay in isolation, with his sandy-gold

147

camel beside him. Sarba thought again how like the animal was to Amber. It was odd. Would she really wish to have her own placid, reliable mount back, rather than be riding a black racing camel, with her arms round Tekran?

Jentiz woke her in the heat of late morning. Tekran was still sleeping. She walked across to the pool and knelt to wash the sleep from her eyes and refresh her hot and sticky skin.

'Am I in the way?' Jentiz smiled. 'Would you like me to turn my back?'

'It's hardly big enough to bathe in, is it? A lick and a promise will have to do.'

She still felt self-conscious, kneeling there in front of him, in her white nightgown. To be sure, it was not very different from the simple dress another girl might wear in the daytime, but she missed the familiarity and formality of her Ring-Holder's robe. She had been so proud of the two red bands around her skirt.

'He's been watching us,' said Jentiz quietly.

She followed his eyes across the oasis. Against the aching brilliance of the sand, she could see the Xerappan now. He was hardly more than a brown silhouette, leaning against the trunk of a palm tree.

'Why is he still there? Why doesn't he go? He's had a drink and a rest. Why doesn't he just saddle up his camel and get going? What's *he* got to be afraid of in the daylight?'

'Perhaps he's a fugitive too. He might be in trouble with the Sorcerer Guard, like us. One of the rebels, maybe.'

The thought made Sarba shiver. Men like that had wrecked her mother's life, reduced her to a ruin of the laughing woman she half remembered, had nearly killed Sarba herself, without compassion.

'Or perhaps he's waiting for us,' Jentiz added.

'Wait for us? Why would he do that?'

'He might not believe what I told him about our being on

the run. He might be waiting to see where we go.'

'The Forgotten City? Will it matter if he finds it?'

'He's a Xerappan. He probably knows about it already. He may have been heading there, anyway.'

'We don't know this desert, do we? Perhaps it's the only place you *can* go from here.'

'My turn to sleep,' Jentiz said. 'Shout straight away if you feel there's anything suspicious at all. No heroics. Better a false alarm than a late one. And take Tekran's knife. Just in case.'

He put into her hand the wicked blade she had used to harvest the dates. In her own pouch was a small knife. Nothing like Tekran's, which was meant to be used as a weapon as well as a tool, in the rare event of a sorcerer being parted from his spell-rod. It must have been a humiliation, she thought, for a sorcerer colonel, governor of a colony, to have to ask a younger officer to lend him his.

Sarba took the knife from him. She thought of sticking it into human flesh and felt sick. 'Thank you. I'll be careful.'

There would be four hours to sit alone, in silence. She checked the position of the sun above the trees. Four hours would be a long time alone, unless Tekran woke before then.

It felt strange to be holding the knife while the men slept.

She ate more dates.

'You could get tired of these,' she murmured to the camels, licking the stickiness from her fingers fastidiously. 'But not just yet. I'm going to need all the energy I can get.'

The fierce blue of the sky was intensifying towards noon. She peered through the palm trunks. It was a relief to see that the Xerappan had lain down to sleep.

She fingered the knife in her lap. Would she really have the courage to use it?

Even though she had had a few hours' sleep, her eyelids were heavy with the heat and the glare of the desert between

149

the trees. Under her breath, she made herself recite the chants of the Ring-Holders, as she had sung them so often on the summit of Mount Femarrat. She would never do that again.

Something flickered on the edge of her vision. She scrambled to her feet in panic. Was it a snake, a scorpion? She knew nothing of what might live out here in the desert, but where there was water and vegetation, there could surely be animal life. Her eyes searched the barred shadows and found the cause.

A small brown bird. A sparrow.

The shock drove the blood back to her heart. Then she laughed breathlessly. The sparrow was the commonest bird in Yadu and, presumably, Xerappo. Why should it not be here, when it could be found everywhere else? There was no gold ribbon, no yellow letter on its leg. Nothing to connect it with that little messenger who had turned her life upside down and made her a fugitive in the desert, on the run for her life.

She watched the sparrow hop almost to her feet. Were there still breadcrumbs from their breakfast? It put its head on one side and regarded her with its bright brown eyes. She held out a hand to it cautiously. But the bird did not fly up to it, as its boldness made her half suspect it would.

Instead, it fluttered away a short distance, to the foot of the next tree. It turned its head to look back at her. Only half understanding, she took a tentative step after it. The sparrow flew on, and settled again. Again, Sarba followed it.

Little by little it coaxed her across the oasis. With alarm, Sarba could see now where it was heading. She was now halfway between the two sorcerers, dim red shapes on the ground, only just within earshot, and, ahead, the stranger with his sandy camel. He seemed to be still asleep, wrapped in his brown robe, his head shrouded in the yellow scarf.

She stopped, scared. She ought not to go any further, even with the knife in her hand. They knew nothing about this Barak. None of them trusted him. She had a sudden horrible thought that she could take the initiative, kill him as he slept, remove the danger.

She knew at once she could not do that. But she could turn back, to Tekran and Jentiz and safety.

The sparrow fluttered on. Little by little it was getting nearer to the Xerappan. Its bright eyes told her it meant her to follow. Even as she scolded herself for her folly, she did.

The sparrow stopped by the last palm tree before the sleeping figure. Sarba crept to join it. The trunk was thicker than many others. She pressed herself close behind it. The sparrow hopped a few steps closer. Sarba peered round the trunk to watch.

The man lay, his mouth half open, his breath loud enough to hear. The yellow scarf had fallen away from his face. Sarba stared in horror.

It was not the same man.

Where his chin had been hidden by a curling black beard, there was now only a fair, straight stubble. This face was thinner, the cheeks fallen in, skull-like, the pale skin tight over his bones. Sarba knew with certainty that if those eyelids opened, the eyes would be blue. This was unmistakably the face of a Yadu. And it was one she knew. She was looking down at a sorcerer, at the one of the investigation team she feared above all others: Vendel.

Chapter Fourteen

Terror trapped her, like a mouse cornered by a cat. If she moved, he would hear her and come horrifyingly awake. If she stayed, he could still wake at any moment and see her. He would know she had discovered his secret. She did not doubt what that would mean.

The knife was in her hand.

She was instantly sure of two things. Despite her terror, she could not kill a sleeping man. And if she waited until Vendel woke, he would freeze her arm with a spell.

A spell? Was Vendel so strong a magician, he could make sorcery work, even out here? He could transform himself into the appearance of a Xerappan. But not, it appeared, in his sleep.

Sarba remembered what Tekran had told her: that the exercise of sorcery was not simply a matter of waving a spell-rod and chanting the right words. The spell must be held in place by the will of the sorcerer. It demanded great strength and energy. Vendel's sunken cheeks told of his exhaustion.

She did not notice the moment at which she decided to retreat. Perhaps it was the thought that Vendel's power was not absolute which made her risk it. She was already taking a cautious step backwards, glancing for the next tree large enough to shelter her. The sand was soft underfoot. She made no noise. Vendel still slept.

She was lengthening the distance. Before long, she would be far enough away to seem to be merely patrolling, if Vendel woke. She made herself turn away from him. To walk in a different direction, not directly to Jentiz and Tekran, though she longed to run to them. It must not be obvious that she was fleeing straight from Vendel to them.

It was terribly hard not to turn her head back to him. Had he woken, even while he continued to lie still? Had his terrifying blue eyes opened into narrow slits, watching her, knowing? What might happen to her, before she reached the others?

The sparrow fluttered some distance from her, between the palms. Though it could not speak to her, the sight of its tiny, fragile brown body held the warmth of friendship.

At last she was at the edge of the oasis, where the shade of the palms gave way abruptly to the glare of the desert. Now she could turn, and walk back to the others by a different route. She still must not hurry. Nothing in her bearing must suggest alarm.

A glance to her left confirmed what she had feared. Vendel was a small figure in the distance, but he was awake. He was pulling the brown robe around him, adjusting the yellow scarf over his face. Sarba did not doubt that he was making a more profound adjustment. When she saw him close to again, the eyes would be dark, the black beard restored. He would be to all intents and purposes the Xerappan, Barak.

Her heart was racing. He was surely watching her now. She felt sick with apprehension.

Someone else was awake. Tekran had had his sleep out, and was getting to his feet. He waved to her. Sarba fought back the urge to run into his arms, to gasp out her shocking news. She made herself walk calmly forward, until she could speak to him in a low voice.

'Please, keep very still and quiet. You mustn't look as though I'm telling you anything important. That man who looks like a Xerappan and calls himself Barak...'

'I don't think any of us believed that was his name, do you?'

153

'He's... You're not going to believe this, but I swear it's true. He's not a Xerappan at all. I saw him close to, while he was sleeping. He'd... changed. He's Yadu. He's a sorcerer. He's... Vendel.'

She saw astonishment, followed by shock, in Tekran's eyes.

'You're sure? It wasn't a trick of the sun in your eyes? We haven't eaten much for a couple of days. You're sure you're not light-headed?'

She shook her head. 'It's not a mistake. I was standing as near to him as to you now. His scarf had slipped. He doesn't really have a beard. And he's fair, not dark. You know what Vendel's face is like.'

'A weasel's skull.'

'Exactly. I couldn't have made that up. No one else looks quite that sinister.'

'We have to tell Jentiz.'

'You believe me, then?'

'Of course. Shouldn't I? There always was something suspicious about the way he appeared, just when we thought we'd got safe away.'

'And he could change his appearance like that, by sorcery?'

'Simple enough, for a sorcerer of his rank, if he's got a spell-rod hidden away under his robe.' He was already moving, careful not to appear to hurry, to where Jentiz lay still sleeping after his early watch.

The colonel came instantly awake. He sat up, his eyes narrowed, focusing on the news they were telling him. Sarba blessed the training of sorcerers, which made them alert immediately to deal with danger, without asking unnecessary questions.

'This Vendel. He must be a powerful sorcerer, to keep up such an illusion out here. You know how we felt our own power weakening, Tekran, so far from Mount Femarrat and the colonies?'

154

'We were all afraid of him on Mount Femarrat, even though he was supposed to be on our side. There were rumours he was powerful enough to hold a much higher rank, but he couldn't be trusted not to use that power in nastier ways than the Sorcerer Guard thought appropriate even for Xerappans. Still, the gossip was that Lord Cozuman would use him if there was a particularly unpleasant job that needed to be done.' Tekran glanced sideways at Sarba. 'I'm sorry. I know he's your father.'

'Lord Cozuman does what needs to be done to keep Mount Femarrat and all Yadu safe.' Her voice sounded harsh, even to herself.

'A powerful sorcerer Vendel may be,' said the colonel, 'but there are limits even to his strength. No wonder he slept as far from us as he could get. Not even he could keep the spell alive while he was asleep.'

'Not without the support of our Control Room on Mount Femarrat, sir. And I guess that can't reach so far beyond the border.'

'All of those shifts of sorcerers in Headquarters, making spells to keep other sorcerers' magic going,' Sarba wondered.

'What did you think?' Tekran flashed a sudden grin at her. 'That we just chanted for several hours a day because we liked the sound of male-voice singing? Well, and the odd female like Innerta. It's really hard work, but without it, Yadu would fall apart.'

'There are more primitive means.' Jentiz got to his feet. He took Tekran's knife from Sarba. She had forgotten she was still holding it.

'Would you...?' Sarba remembered how she had had that one chance, standing over Vendel while he slept.

Tekran reached out. His hand closed over the older man's wrist. 'I think not, sir. We rescued you from prison, because we knew if you stayed, Cozuman would have you killed. Is that what you want us to be like? Is that why Sarba and I threw away the lives we had, to flee into the Xerappan desert?'

Colonel Jentiz looked at him in astonishment. 'You were trained as an officer in the Sorcerer Guard, boy. Are you too soft to kill, if you have to? To save your friends?'

'I was too soft to share responsibility for killing you, when you were seen as an enemy of Yadu.'

Jentiz's face darkened. Sarba was not sure whether it was anger or shame. Perhaps both. 'If he's following us, and hasn't made any move to overpower us yet, it can only mean one thing. He wants to know where we're going. He wants us to lead him to the Forgotten City. He means to capture Alalia.'

'Could he call the Sorcerer Guard from there?' asked Sarba, breathless. 'Would his sorcery be strong enough? Would they know how to follow us?'

They had not escaped, they could not escape. Whatever they did now, her father's Sorcerer Guard would find them. The three of them would betray not only themselves, but Jentiz's daughter and her Xerappan friends.

'What are we going to do? Either we kill him, or… We can't go on, can we? We can't lead them to her.'

'I doubt if there's anywhere else to go,' said the colonel. 'If we don't go on to the Forgotten City, we can either stay here, and die slowly of a diet that consists of nothing but dates, or strike out into the desert in a different direction, and die of thirst. Or,' looking straight at Tekran, 'we kill this Vendel.'

'It's a little late to do it while he's sleeping,' said Sarba. 'He's coming to join us.'

The man was walking towards them through the barred shadows of the palms. Sunlight caught his yellow scarf and brown robe, and then the figure turned dark again. In and out, in and out of the shade, he was changing as he approached.

A shudder ran through Sarba as she saw the dark eyes

through the swathing scarf. Could this really be the same man she had seen sleeping? Surely, anywhere, she would recognize the fair-haired sorcerer Vendel, that lean and hollow look, the menace she had always felt in his still presence? This man was shorter, burlier, the head broader. She glimpsed black curling hair at the side of his face. Could sorcery really do this? Out here?

'Don't try anything with the spell-rod,' Jentiz muttered, low and rapidly, to Tekran. 'He's stronger than we are. Our only hope is to catch him by surprise.'

'Let's not even let him know we suspect.'

Sarba glanced at the two of them. She saw Jentiz sheathe the knife. How could she control her own face and hide the terror she felt of Vendel?

'You're rested, I hope?' The man who looked like a Xerappan, and was not, creased his eyes in a smile. He turned it on Tekran. 'It is not courteous in my country to stare at someone like that.'

Tekran started. 'I'm sorry! I was thinking of something else.'

Be careful, Tekran, be careful. This man may have more power than he is using.

The false Barak turned his intent gaze on her. 'Your bracelet. They say you Yadu Ring-Holders have the power to call down your god in flame. Have you ever tried it, out here?'

She was shocked by the question. Not because it had never occurred to her, but because it had. Neither Jentiz nor Tekran had asked this of her. Yet was it just possible that she could do this, as the Ring-Holders in the colonies did? Could she make a new flame, away from Mount Femarrat, and renew the power of the sorcerers' rods, out here in the desert?

Suddenly, it was as if the disguised Vendel was seeing into her mind. If only she had tried earlier, if she had found a way to strengthen Tekran's spell-rod, he and Jentiz might have met Vendel with equal strength. Now she knew this was no idle question. Vendel wanted her power for himself. The bracelet burned on her wrist.

Her cheeks were burning too. 'That's a strange question for a Xerappan to ask. We have given you reason to fear our power.'

'And so we do. But when life and death are at stake, enemies may find a common cause. I, a Xerappan, have shared my bread with you, who are Yadu. If you have power of another sort, you should share that too. The desert can be a more deadly enemy than either you or I.'

Jentiz turned away. 'There's no need for sorcery. Camels will get us where we want to be.'

The sun was still high on its afternoon path. There must be hours to nightfall. Yet Jentiz started to walk towards their mounts. Sarba and Tekran exchanged alarmed glances, then followed him.

'How will we know where to go without the stars?' whispered Sarba.

'It no longer matters,' he muttered back. 'I'm sorry, Sarba.'

Blood left her face as she understood. Somewhere out there was the Forgotten City and Alalia. Colonel Yekhavu would never lead Vendel to his daughter. So the three of them would ride on into the uncharted desert until they collapsed. Somewhere out there, on a dune like those around her, her bones would lie.

The stranger seemed equally startled. 'You're going now? Before the stars come out?' he called to Jentiz.

'I know my way, thank you. You may wait for nightfall to choose yours.'

But the man rose, and walked swiftly back to saddle his camel. When they left the oasis, he followed.

It was strange to be riding in daylight. Sarba felt uncomfortably exposed. The hot afternoon sun was on her arms, instead of

158

the chill of night. The blue sky was devoid of stars.

It hit her now with the true force of reality. They would lead Vendel away from the Forgotten City. There, Alalia, the Xerappan boy and his sister would live on in peace and freedom. Once, she had thought she too would join that community. She had even shuddered at the thought of living with Xerappans. Now it seemed like a paradise whose gates were closed to her for ever.

The sun was beginning to decline, though it would be a while yet to nightfall. The dunes ahead grew higher. Shadows were beginning to creep down their eastward flanks. Jentiz turned Carnelian's head further north.

Vendel must have sensed that. He urged his camel into a canter and overtook them. 'From the tracks of your camels, this is not the way you were heading last night. Why are you changing direction?'

Jentiz's voice was reasonable, as if faintly surprised. 'Last night, we needed to find the oasis. Our way to it lay west. From here, the city we seek is on a different bearing.'

'City? What city?'

There was a silence. In his attempt to avert one danger, the colonel had said too much.

It was Tekran who answered. 'Surely you, a Xerappan, know that, in the desert, half a dozen nomad tents constitute a city.'

'Is that what you're seeking? A nomad encampment?'

'Do the laws of courtesy in your country permit such a question?' Jentiz found his voice again with the rebuke. 'We told you, you have no need to come with us. You surely didn't set out into the desert without knowing your own destination?'

They faced each other, the tall Yadu colonel and the dark-eyed sorcerer-in-disguise. Then the false Xerappan smiled, and for the first time since she had glimpsed him sleeping,

159

Sarba saw the malice she feared in Vendel's face.

Without a word, he turned his camel, that sturdy, sandy beast who was so like Amber, and headed into the setting sun.

Jentiz gasped. The three looked at each other.

'That's the right way, isn't it?' Sarba whispered. 'The way to the Forgotten City.'

'Perhaps he's bluffing,' said Tekran. 'He thinks we're trying to lead him astray. If he's right, we'll come after him. If he's wrong, we'll hold our new course.'

Jentiz fingered Tekran's knife, which was still in his belt. 'If he keeps going, he'll find them. It can't be far away now.'

'We don't know that.'

'All the same, can I risk letting him go?'

'We have to call his bluff with our own.'

Tekran urged Basalt forward. The black camel bore him and Sarba slowly up the slope of drifted sand. Sarba looked back. Jentiz was hesitating, torn between the soldier's desire to take swift, aggressive action and the governor's training to use diplomacy to avert an impending crisis. Reluctantly, he followed Tekran's lead.

Sarba looked over her shoulder. Vendel and his camel were climbing straight up the dune. The distance between their two tracks was widening. She watched the rear view of the camel and whispered to Tekran.

'That camel he's riding. Does it look familiar to you?'

Tekran followed her gaze. 'No, I can't say it does. One sand-coloured camel is pretty much like another. That one's a bit broad in the beam. Not the racy sort we favour in the Sorcerer Guard... No! Wait!'

'It is, isn't it? It's Amber. The one Sergeant Ilian picked for me. The one you said wasn't exactly the world's most streamlined animal.'

'Did I say that? Well, he's hardly going to win a race against Basalt, is he?'

'But why Amber? Why not his own?'

'Because I know camels. Because Vendel knew if he rode his, I'd recognize it in a flash. Topaz. He's the same colour as your Amber. Well, most camels are. But taller and leaner. And he's got these distinctive black markings around his mouth and nose. I'd have spotted him right away.'

'So he stole poor Amber.'

'He's not one of our regular mounts, not with a girth like that. I don't know where Ilian found him. Vendel probably assumed he was one of the colony's camels. But you're probably wrong that he stole him. I'd be very surprised if Vendel's doing this alone. Colonel Gordoz will have sent him out after us. Once he found us, he'd have orders to communicate our whereabouts back to the colony. And then to tell where we're leading him.'

The shock chilled her. 'Do you mean, they already know where we are? The Sorcerer Guard are coming after us *now*?'

'There's just a chance they aren't. Vendel's power of sorcery is weak here. I don't know if he'd have the strength to transmit a message that far across the desert.'

'Maybe... is that why he's so interested in my bracelet? Why he asked if I could call down the Power, here?'

She felt Tekran tense. 'You think he wanted you to light the flame, so that he could use it?'

'Why else would he risk asking about it, when he's supposed to be a Xerappan?'

They rode on. The fierce blue of the afternoon had gone. The sky was paling, rather than darkening, before the onset of night. The first faint stars stole into view. Soon, Sarba could see the hair of the Mermaid. She was right: the constellation was no longer in front of them.

The distance between Vendel's camel and their own widened further.

Even the lean, long-legged Basalt was labouring now, up the loose sand of the dunes. Tekran made soft, encouraging noises. When Sarba looked to her left again, she had to stare hard before she made out the faint movement of Amber against the sand. Vendel had chosen a shorter route up. He would reach the ridge before they did.

The western sky was glowing with streaks of purple and red. She watched Vendel's figure begin to be silhouetted against it. She felt a wave of affection and pity for the sturdy Amber, hauling him up to the summit.

As they crested the ridge, Amber halted suddenly, pulled up short by his rider. They were too far away for Sarba to hear what cry burst from Vendel. But she saw the sorcerer raise his fist in triumph.

'Tekran! He's seen something!'

Jentiz turned at her cry. Basalt was straining to carry them higher. Bearing the lighter burden of a single rider, Carnelian forged ahead. He reached the crest and a cry of despair broke from the colonel. A few strides more and the others joined him.

They were looking down to where the dunes fell away in wind-rippled slopes to a level plain. The nearer part was red-gold sand, still glowing in the sunset. But in the centre, like an island set in a golden sea, lay a huge oasis. 'City' was not too fine a name for it. This was no encampment of nomad tents. Out of the dark greenery of its trees rose the walls and domed roofs of many houses. And at its centre, a white pyramidal tower so tall it could only mark a palace or a temple.

'The Forgotten City,' said Sarba in a dull voice. 'We were too late to lead him away from it.'

Chapter Fifteen

Vendel urged Amber into a slithering canter down the dunes.

'Stop him!' yelled Jentiz, putting Carnelian to the gallop.

It was hard work for the camels on the shifting, slipping sand. For all his double burden, it was the lean racing animal Basalt who forged into the lead. Clouds of grit were flung up around him. It was hard to see what was happening ahead.

As the purple glow of sunset died beyond the hills, darkness fell swiftly.

Tekran slowed his mount. Sarba peered past him. To her surprise, she made out in the starlight that Vendel had halted Amber. A moment later, she saw why. From the enveloping brown robe he had drawn the all-too-familiar white wand, his sorcerer's spell-rod. He was holding it over his head, pointed at the blazing heavens.

'He's sending a message,' panted Tekran. 'He's telling the Sorcerer Guard where to come.'

'Can't you stop him?'

Tekran drew his own spell-rod. He pointed it at the still-distant figure of Vendel and spoke words of power, which Sarba's ears refused to hear. Still Vendel's arm remained aloft.

'It's no good. My power's too weak.'

'Perhaps his is, too. Maybe his message won't get through.'

Jentiz galloped past them, swifter as the ground levelled into harder sand. The knife was in his hand. Tekran urged Basalt into a gallop after him.

Vendel had lowered his arm, his work done. He turned to

face them and pointed his spell-rod at the galloping Jentiz.

Carnelian and Basalt both drew to a halt.

The yellow scarf still enfolded the man's head, but Sarba made out that the skin of the face within it was paler, the cheeks more cavernous, the eyes light, cold.

'You were right,' said Tekran bitterly. 'It was him all along. And none of us sensed that he was spell-working.'

'He's not pretending now.'

'He needed all the strength he could summon to send that signal. He couldn't hold a transformation as well.'

'You tricked me!' shouted Jentiz. 'You, a brother sorcerer. You got me to lead you to my daughter's refuge.'

'You are no brother of mine, Jentiz Yekhavu. You're a traitor. As is your daughter. And so, it seems, is the daughter of Lord Cozuman himself. I think the Sorcerer Guard will find that particularly... upsetting.'

The cold eyes were on her, chilling her spine.

Jentiz lunged at Vendel. The cadaverous sorcerer swung round. There was a small flash from his spell-rod. The knife tumbled on to the sand.

Sarba was aware of a second flash, weaker, but much nearer. Before her eyes, the stolid figure of Amber tottered. He staggered to his knees and rolled over. The astonished Vendel could only leap clear.

Tekran looked down at his own spell-rod, almost in surprise. 'It worked! Of course, that sort of magic doesn't take nearly as much power as a transformation.'

'Is he all right? Amber, I mean. You haven't hurt him?'

The sandy camel's eyes were closed. He snored.

Sarba began to giggle with relief. Then, strong, invisible hands seemed to grasp her. She was being dragged from her high perch behind Tekran. She was tumbling to the ground. Now she was stumbling across the sand towards Vendel. There was nothing she could do to stop herself.

The sorcerer smiled as she reached him. There was nothing remotely reassuring in that smile.

'Quite so, Sorcerer Tekran. It does not require a great deal of magic to make a beast or a girl move as you want. I have Sarba now. I do not think your spell-rod will be much more use to you.'

Another flash. Tekran cried out in pain. His spell-rod lay in the sand.

'Now, I think, Sarba and I can proceed to the city. What you two do is your affair. If you flee, the Sorcerer Guard will find you, or you will die in the desert. If you stay, I can hand you over along with this nest of traitors.'

He gestured to the walls of the city. In the short time since they first saw it, night had darkened it. A few lights glowed softly above the walls, but the town had rapidly merged into the gloom. Only the tall, pyramidal white tower gleamed faintly above dark treetops.

Vendel began to walk towards it. Sarba went with him. No cords bound her, but she had no choice.

His power is weaker here, she told herself. Every moment he holds me under this spell, his strength is draining from him.

She looked round. It was hard to see in the starlight, but she thought Tekran and Jentiz were following.

Her heart twisted with shame. She was being dragged against her will to the gate of the Forgotten City. Alalia Yekhavu would be inside. She would see Sarba. She would know that the High Sorcerer's daughter had betrayed her refuge.

She had been so curious to meet Alalia. To defy her cousin Digonez took a fine courage. On the edge of her mind was the thought, 'to defy my father'. She pushed it away. It was enough to remember Digonez's fury, when they had met him on the road. Now her cousin would have his revenge on the girl who had so insulted him.

There must be guards on the city gates. Would Vendel change back into his Xerappan disguise to gain entry? Surely, Jentiz and Tekran would shout a warning of treachery as they approached?

Will *I*? Can I? Her heart plummeted, as she realized Vendel could strike them mute in the same way he had overpowered her.

But there are three of us, and he is only one, she argued. His strength must be weakening all the time. Tentatively, she tried to hold her right foot from moving forward the next step. Just for a moment it halted, then it was dragged on again.

'I am stronger than you think,' hissed Vendel.

Their feet made no sound on the sand. There was the faintest snort of breath behind them. It must be Basalt and Carnelian, with Tekran and Jentiz. Perhaps Amber, too, if he was awake.

Suddenly, one of the camels bellowed in surprise. Instantly the dark night around her was alive with movement. Human arms pinioned her limbs even more surely than Vendel's sorcery. A knife blade was at her throat.

Through her terror, she was aware that Vendel had cried out. But there was no flash of sorcery from his spell-rod. Were his arms, too, bound to his sides, unable to wield magic?

There were people all around them. Impossible to count in the darkness. Belatedly, she realized she was free from the spell. If only her arms, and now her legs, were not trussed, she would be able to move as she wished. Vendel must be in too much trouble himself to maintain the spell. Yet she could die any moment from the knife of a stranger. These, she was sure, were not the Sorcerer Guard. They did not even smell like the Yadu.

There was a short, burly figure in front of her. The starlight shone on his face. The catch in her breath was almost a scream. It was the face of someone she had seen coming towards her only a few nights ago at her father's house, holding the leash of a leopard. It was the Xerappan chariot driver.

She was flung over his shoulder and carried ignominiously towards the city.

Slung like this, with her head hanging upside down, Sarba would have found it difficult to see much, even if it had not been dark. There seemed to be a mass of people around her, sweeping her and the others, she guessed, along at great speed. They were silent, as well as swift. There had been a few brisk questions and commands after she was seized, then nothing. Nothing but the laboured sound of breathing as the men ran.

There was that smell, though. Onion-scented breath. It brought back the memory of sitting too close to that Xerappan donkey driver on her last visit to her mother. Their accents had been Xerappan, too. What else could she have expected, out here in the desert? Everything in her revolted at being held against the body of a Xerappan. She fought back the urge to struggle vainly for release.

What would they do with her? These people hated the Yadu so much they had poisoned her mother's friends on the beach, had even tried to destroy children like herself.

There were new smells now, smells she could not put a name to, but which spoke of vegetation growing around her. There was even a whiff of manure. She thought of that city seen from the dunes, like an island in a golden sea of desert, with a level green beach round it. They must have entered the ring of fields.

A voice challenged them, ringing hollowly, as if under stone. A password was spoken. People were pressing closer to her, through a narrow entrance. If this was the city, there were

167

few lights. A subdued glow showed a paved road, drifted with sand, below her. There were many sandalled feet, seen from upside down. Feet which had crept up on them in the dark so silently none of them had noticed.

Inside a building. More lights, briefly. A swift exchange of information between her captor and guards in blue tunics and breeches. She was dumped on the floor.

'Saw them on top of the dunes. We caught them approaching the city. Two Yadu sorcerers and this girl. The fourth is a Xerappan. He wasn't with them when they first appeared, but we captured them together. Keep him under lock and key as well, until we find whether he's a collaborator.'

'Good lad. Tell Rasmullin about this.'

Alalia's chariot driver left the room.

'What's that on her wrist?'

She was jerked violently upright. A hand seized her arm, twisting it painfully sideways against her bonds. There was a sharp intake of breath.

'A Ring-Holder, eh?'

Another dark-bearded face peered into hers.

'What? That's new. And what are *you* doing out here beyond the colonies?'

So they knew, even without her formal robe. She looked round desperately for the others. They were hidden from her by the crowd of Xerappans filling the room.

'I was running away. Because I tried to help Alalia Yekhavu's father. She's here, isn't she?'

The faces surrounding her looked at each other with startled enquiry.

'Novan's girl? The Yadu one, who was meant to wed Lord Cozuman's nephew?'

'Don't trust her. It's a trick. They'd do anything to get their hands on her, after she ditched him.'

'Shall we have that bracelet off her, for a start?'

Sarba tried to keep the horror out of her face. It was ridiculous; her bracelet meant nothing now. She was cast out as a Ring-Holder. Yet it was all that was left of the life on Mount Femarrat which had been so dear to her. Jentiz Yekhavu must have felt like this when they took his spell-rod from him. The Xerappans would take Tekran's, too.

One of the men yanked at the arms lashed together behind her back.

'Nah. We'd have to untie her to get it off. It's only a sort of badge, isn't it? It's not like their blasted spell-rods.'

The weals from the ropes were hurting more than ever, but she blessed the pain now.

'That man you think is a Xerappan,' she said fiercely. 'Don't trust him. He's a Yadu sorcerer too.'

'Oh, yes? With a beard as thick and black as mine? If he's Yadu, I'm a scorpion.'

So Vendel had used his sorcery again. They must not have found his spell-rod.

Her warning sounded futile, even to herself. Since they thought she was their enemy, the Xerappans would not believe anything she said. The more she screamed at them about Vendel, the more they would think he was one of them, a Xerappan. Perhaps that, too, was part of his spell.

She was pushed into a cell. She stumbled and fell full length. The door slammed. She knew there was fear, as well as anger, in their treatment of her. For years, these people had believed themselves safe, two days' journey out into the desert. Her coming here had shown them that even the last refuge of the Xerappans was no longer safe from the Yadu.

Had Vendel truly been able to summon the Sorcerer Guard? How soon would they come, to put an end to the Forgotten City?

Chapter Sixteen

Sarba lay in the darkness, bruised and shaken. Slowly, she sat up. It was awkward; they had released her legs but her arms were still bound. She pressed her knees together to stop her trembling. Gradually she became aware that the darkness was not total. It was suffused with the faintest rosy glow. She could see a little, though there were no lamps, and apparently no windows. It was reassuring to realize that the soft pink light was coming from the bracelet behind her back.

The illumination was dim. She had to get up and walk round her cell to find out what it was like. The walls seemed to be made of large mud bricks, fitted closely together. The floor was beaten earth. Stacked against one wall were lengths of wood. A fragrance of sandalwood stirred when she moved one with her foot. The room was small, enclosed, but it did not seem like a prison cell, more like a storeroom. If she could free her arms, she could, a defiant part of her mind told her, take up one of these pieces of wood and hit the first person who opened the door. She knew immediately that this would not be a good idea.

Where were the others? What was happening to them? How long would it take before they discovered that Jentiz really was Alalia Yekhavu's father? Surely then all would be well?

But how long would it take before they discovered that Sarba was Lord Cozuman's daughter? What would they do to her when they knew?

She did not have long to wait. She had feared that these

Xerappans would not heed her warning, that they would leave her until morning, that she might still be locked in here when the Sorcerer Guard fell on the city.

Instead, they came with lamps: a man in a white tunic with a coarse brown robe, and a woman wearing a long dress striped with blue and purple. She was confused that they did not seem like armed guards.

'The High Council will see you now.'

She was led along a narrow corridor, up steps, into a wider space. A few lamps burned in sockets, but the building had a quiet, night-time air. Her escort knocked at a heavy, carved door.

'Enter.'

The door swung wide into a spacious chamber.

There were more lamps here, but the light was softer than the glare she was used to on Mount Femarrat. Some distance in front of her, four people were seated behind a table: two men, two women. The man in the middle was everything that made her blood run cold when she saw Xerappans, even the servile sort who had stayed on in the land of Yadu. His hair and beard were glossy black, thick and curling. His head and shoulders were broad; even his hands on the table looked blunt and strong. He was all that the tall, slender, fair Yadu were not. The woman beside him was strikingly beautiful. Her black hair fell in softer waves than his, over shoulders draped with a cloak of feathers and fur. She sat taller than he did. As Sarba was led nearer, she saw that the woman's eyes, unusually for a Xerappan, were a vivid blue. They looked at Sarba steadily, thoughtfully.

There was not yet time to take in the others fully: an older woman to one side, smaller and browner, a man at the other end, a thin, stiff figure, with straighter black hair.

'Tell us who you are, and why you are here.' The broad-shouldered man came straight to the point. His dark eyes held hers powerfully.

Sarba's mind flew back over the chaotic events of the last six days. Where should she begin? What was it safe to tell them? How could she convince them that the greatest danger was still to come, and it was not from their captives?

'I was a Ring-Holder on Mount Femarrat. I was sent to the Mount of Lemon Trees to help investigate the... loss... of Alalia Yekhavu. Is she here? I had a message about her for her father.'

'A message? From whom?'

'I don't know. It was brought by a sparrow.' She felt herself blushing. It sounded ridiculous, even to her. She saw the four at the table exchange smiles.

'You tracked Alalia and her Xerappan friends here?'

'It wasn't like that. I'd been sent from... from Lord Cozuman, yes.' She saw the expression of their faces change to hatred and fear at that name. 'But I changed my mind when I met Colonel Jentiz. Tekran and I – he's the young sorcerer with us – we helped Jentiz escape from prison. And the Sorcerer Guard were chasing us. We thought we'd lost them in the desert, only then this other sorcerer appeared. He's disguised as a Xerappan, but you mustn't believe him. It's sorcery that makes him look like that. He's as much a Yadu as the rest of us. He's one of the most feared sorcerers. And I'm terribly afraid he's used his spell-rod to summon the rest of the Sorcerer Guard. They'll find your city. You have to be ready!'

Words were tumbling out of her. How could she expect these Xerappans to make sense of them?

Sarba read consternation and fear in all their faces. The black-haired man turned to the woman in the cloak.

'One of Cozuman's men? *Here?*'

The woman put out a hand to still him.

There was silence. There was something about the angle of the Xerappans' heads that suggested they were listening. But to what? Sarba could hear nothing, now that the man had fallen quiet.

The blue-eyed woman spoke. Her voice was low, but resonant, like bells. 'She is speaking the truth. I hear of great dread in her of the Sorcerer Guard, and of this man – this Vendel – most of all.'

Sarba started. She searched her memory. She did not think she had mentioned Vendel's name. How could this woman know it? Then reason reasserted itself. One of the guards must have told her.

'But there is something else,' the woman went on. 'A different fear which is making her keep something from us.' Her eyes went up to Sarba's, demanding the truth.

Sarba stifled a gasp. This woman already knew too much. It was as if she could see into her mind. What if she discovered whose daughter Sarba was?

The black-bearded man narrowed his eyes. 'Something about her father. She's afraid of him. But she's afraid of something else to do with him, too. She's fighting Searcher. There's something she doesn't want us to know.'

This time Sarba gulped audibly. Who was Searcher? How did he know what was going on in her inmost thoughts?

'Who *is* your father?'

The name rose in her mind. The name she dared not speak.

The thin man on the right of the table rose suddenly, crashing over his chair.

'*Lord Cozuman?*'

There was bitterness in his face. The blue eyes of the woman in the cloak smiled at her astonishingly, as if unsurprised. But Sarba was terrified. How had he known that? How *could* he know?'

The older man thundered at her, 'You're Cozuman's daughter? You confess it?'

Her lip trembled. There seemed no sense in denying it

now. Then she straightened her back and looked defiantly at the Xerappans.

'Yes, I'm Lord Cozuman's only child. But don't think that, because of that, I get any favours, or that there's any special relationship between us. My mother was... poisoned when I was little. My father sent me away from home to be schooled. I was trained as a Ring-Holder. I've never lived with my father since. He treats me no differently from anyone else.'

'Yet he chose you for this mission to the Mount of Lemon Trees? How old are you?'

She coloured. 'Fifteen. But he needed someone young enough to talk to Alalia's friends.'

'To get them to betray her, no doubt.'

She nodded, dumbly.

The tall woman spoke again, in a gentler voice. 'But instead of that, you ran away. With Alalia's father.'

The woman at the other end of the table spoke for the first time. Her voice was brisk. 'Do we know that, for certain? Wouldn't it be a cunning plot to have the governor of the Mount of Lemon Trees come here as a fugitive, when what he really wants to do is wreak punishment on his daughter?'

There was silence again. Again that strange, intent listening.

'I think not,' said the blue-eyed woman quietly. She rose and came towards Sarba. 'Sarba Cozuman, I took a great risk to bring you here. Forgive me.'

The words made no sense.

The woman held out her arms as if to embrace Sarba, but the girl backed away. How could she let herself be held so close by a Xerappan?

'You're wasting time!' she cried. 'Didn't you hear? The Sorcerer Guard are coming!'

Now they were all on their feet. The woman in the cloak turned white.

'Bring Colonel Jentiz!'

'Shouldn't we remove the girl, Rasmullin?' the smaller, brisk woman suggested to the bearded man. 'We don't want them colluding over their stories.'

'There's no chance of that. The Yadu don't have je...' A warning movement from the blue-eyed woman beside him cut him suddenly short. Rasmullin gave a rueful laugh. 'Sorry! They don't have... our resources.'

Before Sarba had time to wonder what this meant, the door opened again. Colonel Jentiz was led in.

She was suddenly aware how travel-stained and weary he looked. The smart crimson uniform, which he had worn with defiant pride even as a prisoner at the colony, was crumpled and sweat-soiled from their flight. He had escaped from one captivity into another. Yet he tried to hold his back erect. His eyes ran keenly over the men and women waiting to interrogate him. He would be assessing the situation, forming plans, readying himself. She felt a warmth of recognition go out towards him. In a short time, she had come to rely on his leadership, his integrity. She made her face form the most encouraging smile she could for him.

'Colonel Jentiz Yekhavu?' Rasmullin began. 'That much can easily be tested. Alalia is here with us now.'

The colonel's face lit up in relief and delight. 'She made it? She's safe?'

The four interrogators looked at each other. They exchanged nods. Their faces relaxed a little.

'Untie the prisoners,' ordered Rasmullin.

They believe him, thought Sarba. It's the first thing he's said, and yet they seem to be sure he's telling them the truth. Is it possible, she began to wonder, that these Xerappans have some magic of their own, after all? The power to read thoughts?

The blue-eyed woman rose and held out her hand to Jentiz. 'My name is Gamatea, Colonel. I am Chief Guardian of the sanctuary in this city. This is Rasmullin, Defender of the City. And these, our deputies. Zana,' she nodded at the brown-haired woman, 'assists Rasmullin, and Urdu,' smiling at the stiff, unresponsive figure on her other side, is second in responsibility to me in the temple. We are grateful to you for your kindness to the Xerappans in your settlement.'

Rasmullin took over. 'As a fugitive from Yadu and the wrath of Lord Cozuman, like your daughter, be welcome to our Forgotten City. You have brought the High Sorcerer's own daughter, as Gamatea hoped you would. But it seems you have also brought on us a terrible danger.'

'I know!' The words were wrenched from Jentiz. 'When I found that Vendel had tracked us, I tried to lead him away. We would have perished in the desert, all of us, rather than betray your city... and Alalia. But we were too late. I didn't know how close we already were. When he saw the Forgotten City...'

'He summoned the Sorcerer Guard. That, at least, is what Sarba believes.' Gamatea spoke quietly, but there was no mistaking the fear in her voice.

'Is there anything you can do to defend yourselves? I'll help, if I can. They took my spell-rod away when they arrested me in the colony, but Tekran still has his.'

'Tekran is the young man who was taken with you? Another of your sorcerers?'

'He came to the Mount of Lemon Trees with me,' said Sarba. 'It was Tekran's idea to rescue Jentiz. He couldn't stand the idea that my father might have him publicly executed. And he would have done, if he thought that it was the way Jentiz brought Alalia up which made her break off her betrothal to my cousin.'

'Tekran has been relieved of his spell-rod. I can assure you of that,' Rasmullin told them.

'But you could give it back,' Jentiz said. 'Or give it to me. I don't promise it will be much help. The further we get from Mount Femarrat, the weaker our power grows. Unless Sarba can...' He looked at her appealingly.

She fingered her Ring-Holder's bracelet and said nothing. When she looked up, she saw that Gamatea was gazing intently at her with those vivid blue eyes.

'It's Vendel whose sorcery you have to fear,' insisted Jentiz. 'He's in a different league from the rest of us. And I'm terribly afraid we may be running out of time.'

'There is little we can do against your Sorcerer Guard,' said Gamatea. Still she did not raise her voice, but there now was an edge of bitterness in it. 'As you know. How else did you win the war and take half our country from us? Why can we not prevent you, even now, crossing the border and building a colony on every hilltop? Only the desert is left to us. I was foolish to hope we would remain safe, even here. I had hoped to use Sarba Cozuman for good. But I fear, instead, I have brought a terrible wrong on this city. I did not think the Sorcerer Guard would follow so hard on your heels.'

The urgency in the room was mounting. Two things happened quickly. Tekran was led in. This time, Sarba's joy was so great, she rushed across the room to meet him, then stopped, blushing. He threw her a broad, rueful smile.

Almost at the same time, there were more quick footsteps at the door. A tall, fair girl ran into the room. She showed none of Sarba's inhibitions. She flung herself into Jentiz's arms.

'Papa!'

His arms were round his daughter, straining her tight. They hugged each other wordlessly. Two blond Yadu embracing, in a room full of dark Xerappans. At last he put her away from him.

'So? You decided the match your mother and I made for you was not to your liking? It would have saved us both rather a lot of trouble if you'd said so before you left home.' He even managed a smile for her, though his voice shook a little.

'I didn't know then how horrible Digonez is. If you'd seen what he did to me, the night before our betrothal. He humiliated me in public!' She shuddered. Then she turned to the door. Her face lit up with a rosy blush. 'I could never have escaped him by myself. Papa, I want you to meet Novan. He isn't our servant now. He's a free man.'

Sarba turned too. There were two more people behind her, both Xerappans. The chariot driver, who had flung her, captive, over his shoulder. He was a teenager, sturdy and dark, like Rasmullin, probably, when he was younger. And a smaller girl, with curling black hair and an impudent smile.

'And this is Mina,' Alalia went on. 'His sister. She helped me escape.' Her expression changed. 'Oh, Papa, have you heard what happened to Balgo? What he did?'

Jentiz nodded, grief overcoming his new-found joy. 'I gather there was a battle of sorcery between Digonez and your brother. Not surprisingly, Balgo lost.'

'He did it for us. He saved our lives. He was so brave! I never even guessed he was such a good sorcerer. But, no, he wasn't good enough to win. Digonez killed him.'

They hugged each other again.

'But this young man… Novan? … got you away?'

'Him and his jerboa. Well, Mina's too.'

There was an intake of breath around the room, and then a hush. Alalia looked round at all the Xerappans' faces. They showed alarm, even horror.

'I'm sorry! Shouldn't I have said…?' The Yadu girl looked conscience-stricken.

Then Sarba saw all the Xerappans' eyes focus on something at Novan's feet. Sarba looked down too.

She had hardly noticed the blue-and-white tiles of the floor until now. But there was something small and brown there as

178

well. A mouse, she thought, startled. But why was it sitting up like this, looking boldly back at all those staring faces? It might almost have been smiling. And then she saw that this was no household mouse. The ears were far too large, gleaming pinkly. The eyes were huge and black. The spindly hind legs were impossibly long for its body.

'That's a jerboa, isn't it?' said Tekran. 'A sort of desert rat?'

'His name's Thoughtcatcher,' said Novan quietly.

And Sarba was aware, with a prickling of her skin, that jerboas were emerging from all over the room. Mina's was piebald, black and white. Rasmullin's was brown, bigger than Thoughtcatcher. Gamatea's was pure white. Every Xerappan seemed to have one. Even the Yadu girl, Alalia, drew out of her sleeve a shy little brown-and-white animal.

Gamatea said, looking steadily at Jentiz, '*These* are our only defence.'

Sarba drew a deep breath. 'That's how you did it! When Rasmullin talked about Searcher, *that's*,' pointing at the large jerboa, 'what he meant. That's how you got inside my mind.'

'Exactly so,' affirmed Gamatea. 'We had not intended to reveal our secret to you so soon. Not until we were sure how far we could trust you. But Thoughtcatcher seems to think the time is too short to play games with each other and the danger too great.'

Again that listening silence. No matter how hard Sarba strained, she could hear nothing. But the Xerappans obviously could.

'Call the man these Yadu say is the sorcerer Vendel,' ordered Rasmullin, 'though he looks like a Xerappan and says his name is Barak. We need the truth.'

Chapter Seventeen

The room was abuzz with questions. At the table, the four Council leaders conferred urgently. Alalia and her father were bombarding each other with questions. Alalia dragged the young Xerappan boy forward.

'I hope you won't be too cross with me, Papa. Novan and I are... well, we're betrothed. Sort of. Under Mount Femarrat there's an ancient Xerappan sanctuary.'

'It had marvellous pictures, of a Xerappan king and a Yadu queen, reigning side by side,' Mina, Novan's sister, cut in excitedly.

'When we thought Digonez was going to kill us, Novan and I decided we wanted to be like those two, even if it was the last thing we did.'

'Balgo and I did it,' cried Mina. 'We threw the water from the sacred pool over them and said the words. They promised to love each other. And then Balgo finished it off when we went under the water and got into the Jerboas' Nest.'

Jentiz shook his head, laughing. 'I can't understand half of what you're all talking about. I know about the summit temple, but I've never heard anything about a sanctuary *under* Mount Femarrat. The one thing that seems to be clear to me is that this young man saved you from Digonez and you intend to marry him.'

'Something like that,' smiled Alalia. 'You've got the important bit.'

'Who are you?'

Sarba looked down, startled. At her elbow was the small figure of Mina, grinning up at her with bright brown eyes.

'Have you run away from the Yadu sorcerers, like Alalia?'

'Yes,' said the Ring-Holder. Fear held back her tongue from answering the first question. She knew for certain how the truth would change the atmosphere. It had happened already with the Council leaders. It would be the same with Novan's sister, with any Xerappan. To tell the truth, to confess that she was the High Sorcerer's daughter, would provoke shock, incredulity, fear. How could she ever live here as one of them, even if she wanted to?

Before she had time to speak, the atmosphere in the room changed suddenly. The sober conferences and excited chatter fell still. Out of the corner of her eye, Sarba caught a quick scamper. She saw the piebald jerboa leap into Mina's sleeve. When she looked round, every jerboa had vanished from sight. The Xerappans were tense, heads up, looking at the door. The four Yadu were caught by surprise.

Sarba felt the chill of her sinking heart. The man who was led in between two burly Xerappan men looked very much like them. The same blunt features, curling black hair and beard. The same broad shoulders beneath a coarse brown robe. The yellow scarf had been pushed away from his face. His hands, she noticed, were not bound.

She clenched her fists until the nails bit into her palms. He's having to use sorcery to keep up the disguise, she told herself. As long as he holds it, it's draining his strength. He won't be able to do much else in the way of spells.

Why hadn't they taken his spell-rod from him, like Tekran's?

The four leaders behind the table looked at him steadily. Their faces showed nothing of the panic they should be feeling, with one of the Sorcerer Guard so close.

'Your name?' asked Rasmullin.

'Barak.'

181

A swift lift of the Defender of the City's hand forestalled any protest the other Yadu newcomers might have made.

'And what brings you to the Forgotten City? We do not know you.'

The smile that opened in the man's beard had something of the menace of Vendel's. 'I learned that two Yadu sorcerers and a Ring-Holder were heading out into the desert, looking for you. They're on a mission from Mount Femarrat, sent by the High Sorcerer himself. He must have got wind that we had a last refuge, out here in the desert. He intends to find and destroy it. That girl,' swinging suddenly round on Sarba, 'is Lord Cozuman's daughter!'

Not one of the Councillors' faces betrayed that they knew this. But the consternation in the looks of Alalia, Novan and Mina told Sarba everything she needed to know. They were staring at her with horror.

'I tracked them,' went on the false Xerappan. 'I hoped I might be able to steer them away from you, or failing that, to kill them before they got to you. As your men will tell you, I was struggling with them when they seized us. Unfortunately, I was one against three, and they had spell-rods.'

'Yet you remained unharmed? They didn't use a slay-spell on you?'

The man blustered a bit. 'I took them by surprise. I made the young one drop his rod.'

Gamatea whispered in Rasmullin's ear. The message was passed along the table.

There was a silence. The four were gazing hard at this man who said his name was Barak. No word was spoken to him. The rest of the room waited uneasily. Then Sarba saw curious smiles light the faces of Novan and Mina. They glanced at each other, as though they hugged a secret. Sarba herself caught Tekran's eye. He shrugged. Evidently he did not understand what was happening, either.

At last, Gamatea spoke. 'You did not answer our question.'

'What question?'

'The one we have been putting to you for several minutes.'

'You said nothing. You've just been staring at me in silence. What was I supposed to answer?'

The smiles that passed between the four Councillors were grim, but satisfied.

'If you couldn't hear the question, you're not a Xerappan,' said the little brown-haired woman, Zana.

Belatedly, Sarba understood. Of course! The Xerappans had been asking him silent questions through their jerboas. If he had been a true Xerappan, he would have had his own little mind-reader. He would have known their thoughts, and answered them with his own.

She felt a wave of relief. Living out here, beyond the reach of sorcery until now, it would not have been surprising if the Councillors had doubted her story. They might well have believed that Lord Cozuman's daughter would try to trick them. They might have thought that a man who looked so convincingly like a true Xerappan must be telling the truth. But the jerboas knew.

A moment later, she flinched from the fury in Vendel's face. He had looked round in bewilderment at the Xerappans surrounding him. He saw only the mixture of scorn and hatred they turned on him. He had no way of knowing what they meant, how he had been supposed to read their thoughts. Nothing had been said about jerboas; no little creature had reappeared. The Xerappans meant to keep their secret from him as long as they could.

But I know, Sarba thought. They trust me. I could tell him, if I wanted to.

It had not been the Xerappans who had first trusted her. It was their jerboas. She pictured them sitting up with their quivering whiskers and big pink ears, their bright eyes fixed on her. They had read her mind. They had known she was telling the truth. They had let her see them. She felt enormously grateful.

She was abruptly jerked out of her thoughts. A hand closed, vice-like, round her wrist. Vendel was dragging her towards him. To her horror, she saw that he had changed. Right in front of her face was the cadaverous Yadu sorcerer, the sight of whom had always filled her with dread. He had cast aside the transformation-spell which no longer protected him. She quailed before the intensity of those pale blue eyes.

Why didn't the Xerappans leap to restrain him? Why did Tekran appear to be fighting his way towards her, and yet getting no closer? Why were she and Vendel standing alone with a ring of alarmed people round them, separated by a circle of blue-and-white tiles they seemed unable to cross?

Vendel was holding something in his other hand. Something very small, slender and white, tipped with gold. He was pointing it at the Xerappans and the other Yadu, swinging it round, so that it menaced all of them. Just as if it were his spell-rod.

She swallowed hard, as she caught the truth. This *was* his spell-rod. It was no bigger than the pin with which one might fasten a cloak. Vendel must have known the Xerappans would search their prisoners for weapons, even one who looked like them. He had transformed not only his own appearance, but the rod on which his sorcery depended. They would not have noticed it, stuck through the brown fibres of his robe.

Vendel was bending her arm painfully, forcing it up towards him. What was he doing?

He brought his other hand, gripping the tiny spell-rod, to hers. The Ring-Holder's bracelet burned on her wrist. She gasped with shock. He was inserting the little white wand into the carnelian ring.

'Call down fire!' he hissed at her. 'You can, can't you?'

'I don't know! I've never tried.'

'Try now!'

The pain was intense. It was as though the rod were indeed a pin, driven deep into her wrist. She fought down the urge to scream.

'We're not in a sanctuary. There's no copper bowl, no oil, no Stone.'

'Trappings, toys. All I need is the flame.'

Need for what? But she knew. His power was not at full strength, because they were too far from Mount Femarrat. Yet she had seen in the colony how that power could be extended beyond the border. It could reach out even into the desert if the flame were summoned.

If *she* summoned the flame. Once or twice on their flight she had wondered if that were possible. If this bracelet were more than just the insignia of her rank. If she carried that latent power.

Her bracelet and Vendel's spell-rod. With a chilling certainty, she knew it could be done. If only she and Tekran had tried it, while he still had his rod!

Thoughts tumbled over each other in her frantic mind. There had been a reason why she hadn't wanted to summon the Power. It was because it was not just they who could draw on it, but the whole Sorcerer Guard pursuing them. She had made the decision to abandon her power.

'No,' she said, clenching her muscles against the agony. 'I won't. You want to call the Sorcerer Guard, but I won't let you.'

'Oh, it's too late for that. I've already signalled them. They should be here quite soon.'

She threw a desperate look at the ring of faces surrounding her. Was there no one who could help her? Did the Xerappans have no spells, no weapons, against this? Was there nothing their thought-reading jerboas could do?

A slow, heart-stopping movement caught her eye. Just inside the door was a man who had not been there before. He was drawing a bow, sighting along the arrow. She saw the blue feather against his cheek.

There was a *zing*, which might be the last thing she heard. The arrow hovered in the air in front of her, then fell with a light clatter on the blue-and-white floor. She did not need to look at Vendel's face to picture his malevolent smile.

'You couldn't win a war against Yadu sorcery last time with bows and arrows. Have you not learned anything from your defeat? The sorcerers are going to take this city, as we've taken everything else which you once called yours. There is nothing you can do to stop us.'

Through waves of pain, Sarba was aware that Gamatea was leaving the room.

'Summon the flame, you little idiot!'

She felt Vendel's mind bearing down on hers. She had never been so afraid of him. His secretive face, with that intense stare of his cold blue eyes, had always sent shudders down her spine. He made her feel that she must be guilty of some crime against the Sorcerer Guard of Yadu, and that he alone would smell it out and punish her.

Now she had a new horror. All the power of Vendel's sorcery was bent on forcing her will to comply with his. He would make her want what he wanted, do what he would do. She would no longer be herself.

She could feel his miniature spell-rod being thrust further through her bracelet, pressing into her flesh. It was cold, where the bracelet was warm.

There was a sudden shock, which made both her and Vendel cry out. Had there been a flash of light, or was it an explosion in her brain? Waves of stronger heat were coming from the bracelet, washing over her. But they were no longer intense pain. It was a kind of ecstasy, a thrill she had never felt before. Vendel must be feeling something like this too. He was whispering intensely over her head.

'Power, yes, the Power!'

The crowd surrounding them was drawing back, closer and closer to the walls, as if the room seemed too small for them to escape these two. Were they frightened of her, as well as Vendel?

Then she knew. There *was* power. She could feel it coursing through her. Now the rod and the ring were joined, sorcerer to Ring-Holder, white to red, cold to heat, something new had been made. She was part of it. She was equal to Vendel. It was her power, as much as his.

She felt his will beating against her mind. *The flame. Call down the flame!* But she no longer cared. She was no longer his creature, his prisoner. She had a will of her own. She could use this power how she wished.

But only as long as she was linked to Vendel. Only if she could master his will and bend it to hers, as he was trying to impose his on her.

The glory shrivelled. She was not truly free. Power was hers only as long as she shared it with Vendel. He would use it to destroy all this. She looked round the room, at the fearful, staring faces. At Tekran, looking at her as if she were a stranger. At Colonel Jentiz, anxiously reaching out for his daughter. At Novan, already by Alalia's side; at the dark, nervous eyes of Mina. At Rasmullin and his fellow Councillors, bracing themselves for a last, desperate stand.

Now Vendel had changed his grip. He was forcing her other hand down to her bracelet. As it touched the warm carnelian she felt a renewed shock.

'Yes!' Vendel hissed. *'Yes, now!'*

Sarba's fingers curled. The tips of them crept under the rim of the bracelet. She felt simultaneously its heat and the chill of the sorcerer's spell-rod. She could do it, now. And when she did, nothing would ever be the same.

Her fingers tightened. There was very little room between the bracelet and her wrist. It hurt. Far more, she felt the colossal hurt of what she was about to do. She could not know the consequences. The life and death of many people hung on her decision.

Now!

She wrenched suddenly. There was the tiniest *crack*, which sounded to her as if the universe were splitting apart.

The bracelet broke.

Chapter Eighteen

There was the tiniest clatter as Vendel's spell-rod dropped on the tiles. It lay there, intersecting the blue-and-white pattern, no bigger than a cloak-pin. Scattered to either side were the two rosy fragments of Sarba's ring.

She stared at it. In the moment of realizing the extent of her power, she had thrown it away.

Vendel swore, but his hands were empty. His curses had now no strength. There was a swirl of his brown robe as he let go of Sarba and swooped for the floor. But his spell, which had held the crowd back, was broken. All round the sorcerer and Ring-Holder people rushed forward.

Novan was the quickest. He snatched up the little rod, before Vendel's hand could close over it. Even as he grasped it, the spell of diminution faded. The rod returned to its normal size.

Rasmullin and his guards seized the sorcerer. He struggled dementedly, but without sorcery his physical strength was as nothing to theirs.

Sarba collapsed on the floor, weeping for the loss of something she could not yet begin to comprehend. She was aware of Tekran bending over her, kneeling beside her, his arm round her shoulders.

'Sarba, Sarba, that was so brave. Don't cry. You did what no one else could do. You broke his power.'

She sniffed and sat up. 'You don't know what it felt like. It was my power, too. Just for a few moments, I knew I could do anything. Now, I've lost it. I'll never be a Ring-Holder again, and I've only just found out what that could mean.'

'When they trained us as sorcerers, they didn't say anything about putting a spell-rod and a ring together. We thought you were just there to call down the Power in the sanctuary, so that we could light the flame.'

'We thought that *we* were the ones who lit the flame. We just invited you to join in with your spell-rods, so that you wouldn't be jealous of us. We thought you were really just a glorified police force, with special weapons.'

'Now we know there's more to it than that. There are other spell-rods, other rings. Someone could do that again.'

Sarba shivered, and he drew her close.

'Who will it be, next time? What will they do with that power?'

'Tekran.' A woman's voice spoke over their heads.

They both looked up. It was the Chief Guardian of the city's sanctuary, which must be that white temple with sloping walls, which looked so like Mount Femarrat.

'We owe you our thanks, Tekran. You saved Jentiz Yekhavu, who is our friend… and Sarba.'

She was holding something out to Tekran.

He gasped with joy. It was his spell-rod. He reached out an eager hand to take it. It looked impressively large, compared with the shrunken pin under which Vendel had disguised his own. Tekran's was as thick as his thumb, and as long as his arm from wrist to elbow; polished white, like the purest ivory, tipped with gold. He ran his fingers lovingly over it.

Sarba felt a curl of jealousy. She retrieved the broken halves of her bracelet and slipped them into the pocket of her cloak. She felt certain it could never be mended.

'Of course,' said Tekran, 'it's not a lot of good here. The power of sorcery was weakening, as soon as we left the colonies. Without the Ring-Holders' flame, we can't really operate. It took a powerful sorcerer like Vendel to hold a spell out here, and even his powers were limited.'

'If the Sorcerer Guard come against us,' Gamatea said grimly, 'this may be all we have between us and destruction.'

His eyes flew to her face. 'You'd want me to use sorcery? You, a Xerappan? You'd trust a Yadu sorcerer to defend you?'

'What choice do we have? Vendel was right. We lost the war against you when you invaded, because you had the weapons of sorcery and we did not. Some of us did not choose to fight on. We fled to the desert to live in peace, and left others to wage a resistance campaign in the conquered territories. There is nowhere else for us to run. Either we defend the Forgotten City or we must leave Xerappo for ever. There's nothing else left.'

'Do you think,' said Sarba, 'the Sorcerer Guard is really coming? Could Vendel have sent a message all that way across the desert? He said he needed the power of my ring.'

'You said yourselves, this Vendel is one of your most powerful sorcerers. We must assume his signal got through. We should go to the watchtower, now.'

Rasmullin was giving urgent orders. Armed men and women were coming and going with rapid strides. Gamatea spoke to him. He nodded, and she beckoned to her deputy. Urdu's stiffly controlled face gave little away, but Sarba felt that he looked at her and Tekran with dislike. It was hard to blame him. If Alalia had not fled here, if they and Jentiz had not followed her, the Xerappans would still be living at peace in their Forgotten City.

Yet Gamatea had spoken, inexplicably, as if it was she who had summoned Sarba.

They followed the two Guardians through the busy corridors. Sarba's heart twisted to see the bows and arrows, the swords and armour, the Xerappans were preparing. They would not be the slightest use against sorcery, if Colonel Gordoz and Examiner Orzad had their full powers.

191

But would they? Might they not, too, be weakened by the mile upon mile of desert?

A chill crept round her heart. What if Hania was with them? She could bring that portable copper bowl and the flask of oil, which she had been so insistent that Sarba carry. What if she called down the flame, outside these walls, as Sarba had refused to do for Vendel?

They were hurrying through early sunshine now, in and out of the shade of flowering shrubs and trees. The white temple loomed in front of her. It must be a temple, she was sure of that. Giant statues guarded the entrance: two jerboas, huge images of the little living things, like Thoughtcatcher, who had stared at her with his round black eyes, and read her mind and trusted her. She felt a tremor of awe as she passed through the low doorway between them.

It was shadowy inside, blinding her sun-dazzled eyes for several moments. Around her, columns like the trunks of palm trees were carved into fronds of leaves at the high, slanting ceiling. A sense of space and quiet. Further off, between the columns, the floor in the centre glinted strangely, reflecting the gleam of sparse lamps.

She hurried after the swish of Gamatea's robe along the side wall.

Gamatea spoke in a low voice to someone. There was a small door in a corner of the hall. The Guardian beckoned them after her through it.

Stairs, narrow and angled. The roof sloped in over Sarba's head.

She had not realized how weary she was. And still the steps went on, turning sharply at each corner of the pyramid. The space was narrowing. It was hard not to feel vertigo as the walls sloped ever inwards. She felt she must topple down to the floor far below.

A flash of brilliant sunlight. Gamatea had opened a door.

They stepped out on to the roof. So far had the angled walls of the tower leaned in that the rooftop was far smaller than the broad base. A parapet girdled it. Around this was walking a young woman carrying a horn. She stopped when she saw the door open. Gamatea lifted her eyebrows.

'Any signs?'

'Nothing, madam. The desert looks quiet on all sides.'

The Chief Guardian ran her eyes around the blinding sea of sand which surrounded the oasis city. On three sides they could see for miles. To the east, the way Sarba, Tekran and Jentiz had come, a ridge of dunes foreshortened the view.

'If they come,' said Gamatea, staring at it, 'that's where it will be.'

The young woman with the horn resumed her quiet patrolling, but she paused longest at the eastern wall, gazing at the dunes with narrowed eyes.

'How long?' Sarba forced the words through dry lips. 'How long do you think it will be before something happens?'

Gamatea's black eyebrows rose again. 'Surely, I should ask you that? You came from the Mount of Lemon Trees, as they will. How long did it take you?'

'Two nights travelling. We hid in the daytime. The Sorcerer Guard won't do that.'

'Yet it took a little time before this... Vendel... found you?'

'It was the second day. We were at the oasis.'

'And you think he signalled to his masters straight away?'

'I don't know. The power of sorcery was weakening.' She turned to Tekran. 'You couldn't use your spell-rod as normal, could you? Even the colonel was finding it difficult.'

'The further we got from Mount Femarrat, the harder it was. Mount Femarrat could easily protect the whole of Yadu, but the sanctuaries at the colonies only covered the other settlements in sight of them. Out in the desert, their power soon faded.'

'Protected!' said Gamatea bitterly. 'Is that what you call it? You conquer our country and you talk as if it were *you* who needed protection.'

'I'm sorry.' Tekran flushed. 'We were brought up to believe that the land of Yadu was rightly ours, that you Xerappans were keeping us out of it. That's what the High Sorcerer told us.'

'Though we'd lived there longer than you had? And the hills beyond the border, and this desert? They're yours by right too? You would leave us nothing?'

'I said I'm sorry. I'd never been across the border before. I hadn't seen. It wasn't until I met Colonel Jentiz… He looks at Xerappans in a different way.'

'That's why he was in prison,' said Sarba in a small voice.

'That's why I set him free,' said Tekran.

Gamatea looked at them both for a long moment. 'I owe you an apology. You two risked your lives to do what you have done. Indeed, your lives, with all our lives, are still very much at risk.'

'We brought them here,' Sarba burst out. 'You were living safely in your Forgotten City, and now it's not a secret any more. We tried to lead Vendel away into the desert, but we were too late. He rode to the top of the dunes and saw this.'

'No, Sarba,' said Gamatea, her face masked with sadness. 'It was I who brought you here. I sent the sparrow to you with the letter for Jentiz, in the hope that you would then follow him here. I need you, Sarba Cozuman. You are the High Sorcerer's child. Only you can bring about the change in him which has to happen.'

Sarba stared at her, open-mouthed.

'I knew the risk.' Gamatea's vivid blue eyes were grim. 'But the desert is vast. I did not really think the Sorcerer Guard would be able to track you out here. I was wrong. Still, it is done. We have to think how we can save ourselves. It may not be possible.'

She stared again at the unmoving horizon. Then she

shrugged. 'I don't even know what I'm expecting. A troop of men on camels? A flight of dragons? Little sand-snakes, perhaps, wriggling across the desert in the dusk? How does the Sorcerer Guard attack its prey?'

'I can't tell you, I'm afraid,' said Tekran. 'I'm only in my second year. I've never taken part in such an offensive.'

'We're all of us in unknown territory. The Sorcerer Guard too, perhaps.'

'It's not Colonel Gordoz I'm most afraid of,' said Sarba. 'He's a military sort of man. It's Orzad, the Examiner. He doesn't even wear the sorcerer's uniform. He works differently. He thinks differently. I think my father and he are very close.'

'And what would your father do in these circumstances?'

'I hardly know him. I only know he hates you for what you did to my mother.'

There was a silence. Sarba became aware of being watched by something which was not Gamatea, nor her deputy, Urdu, nor Tekran. She looked down. The Guardian's white jerboa was sitting upright at her feet, gazing up at Sarba. Though she could hear nothing, she knew her thoughts were being read. The jerboa was passing those vivid, painful memories to Gamatea.

At last the older woman spoke, in a voice deep with pity. 'I could say you invaded us. That you killed and damaged so many of our own people. That we have suffered far more than you. But that does not make it right. We harmed ourselves when we harmed your mother, and killed her friends. That is not how the paintings tell us it should be between the Yadu and the Xerappans. We did not receive love, so we did not give love. We are both wounded.'

Then she shook her hair back and straightened her shoulders. 'Well, there is nothing to see here. The horn will warn us.' She led the way back to the staircase.

It was even more vertiginous going down. Sarba could see all the way through the central well to the distant, softly shining floor. She let her hand rest on Tekran's shoulder in front of her, for reassurance.

They had almost reached the bottom when she was aware of a disturbance below. People were trying to come up. Peering round Tekran, Sarba saw the Xerappan brother and sister, Novan and Mina, with Alalia and Jentiz in the rear.

'Is there any news?' Novan called.

'No, or the horn would have sounded. We saw nothing.'

'And we have just two spell-rods?' Jentiz was holding what could only be Vendel's.

'And no bracelet,' said Sarba painfully.

Those below were turning back, making room for the others to descend. They were back in the pillared hall of the temple. Tekran had drawn out his own spell-rod and was fingering it. His face was thoughtful.

'Is there anything you can do?' Sarba whispered. 'Would it have made any difference if I hadn't broken my ring?'

He managed a lopsided grin. 'It might have given *me* more power, but just think how it would have helped the Sorcerer Guard when they came. No, we're probably better off as we are. The odds are just a little bit more equal.'

Unless Hania comes too, and lights the flame, Sarba thought. She dared not tell Tekran that. Unlike the Xerappans, he had no jerboa to read her thoughts.

Sarba's eyes were becoming adjusted to the dim light. She was aware that the others were moving away to the centre of the shadowed space. She sensed restlessness in them all, tension, dread, waiting for something to happen, yet not knowing what. She moved across to join them for comfort.

They were clustered in front of something. She could not see what. It seemed to be on the floor, for they were all looking down. Mina was talking excitedly.

196

'You've got one here! Like under Mount Femarrat! Can you…?'

Gamatea held up her hand suddenly in a warning gesture. Mina's tongue seemed to trip over the next word. Her hand flew to her face. Then she looked round at Jentiz, and at Sarba and Tekran approaching.

'I'm sorry! I didn't think.'

Sarba felt the rejection. No matter what they had just done, the dangers they had braved, they were still Yadu. Still a sorcerer and a Ring-Holder. It was a bitter irony to have broken her bracelet to save the Xerappans from Vendel, and yet still to be seen as an enemy because she had once worn it.

Only now could she see, between the figures in front of her, what they were talking about.

The glow of distant lamps was reflected softly in the smooth, level surface. It was not polished tiles. It was water. A circular pool, dark, whose bottom she could not see.

Like a pool, under Mount Femarrat? She had never heard of that. The High Sanctuary of the Ring-Holders was on the summit of the sacred mountain. Black pillars surrounding a dazzling white platform. A massive block of red Stone, a copper bowl. Fire from heaven. She knew of no way *under* the mountain. What had Mina spoken of? The Jerboas' Nest?

There was no time to wonder. Thin and shrill, a horn sounded from the tower rooftop. Gamatea and Urdu gasped. In the blink of an eyelid, a large grey jerboa leaped from the deputy Urdu's feet and bolted up the stairs. They waited for agonizing moments.

The little creature came bounding back. He crouched tensely in front of them on his long, spindly legs, whiskers trembling. The Xerappans bent over him, breath held. Even Alalia seemed to be listening. In the distance, there were cries of alarm, the clash of weapons. In the hall, Sarba could hear only the silence of held breath.

197

Gamatea looked up. She caught the eyes of Jentiz, Tekran and Sarba, desperate for news.

'It is what we feared. Your sorcerers are coming.'

Chapter Nineteen

'*How* are they coming?' cried Jentiz.

'A number of camels are cresting the dunes at the gallop.'

Jentiz seemed to relax just a little. 'Not a flight of dragons, then?' He even managed a grim smile.

Sarba cried out. 'So there are limits on their sorcery!'

'Let's not get too excited,' Tekran warned. 'Remember what Vendel could do with his spell-rod, even here. We're up against some of the most powerful sorcerers Lord Cozuman could send.'

Sarba was aware that the balance of power had changed. The Xerappans were now listening to the Yadu, watching their faces, relying on their judgment. For years, they had lived in fear of the Sorcerer Guard, but these fugitives had little first-hand knowledge of their enemy.

There was a clatter on the steps outside. Rasmullin burst in, accompanied by several more Xerappans. They were armed and armoured.

Gamatea quickly relayed the news. Rasmullin had scarcely heard her out before he was bounding up the stairs of the tower to see for himself. Gamatea signalled to the Yadu.

'Colonel Jentiz, Tekran, you go with him. You understand better than anyone what these sorcerers might do.'

The two men in their red uniforms ran for the tower. Novan, Alalia and Mina raced after them. Sarba started to follow.

'No, Sarba,' the Chief Guardian called her back. 'Mina, I need you, too.'

The girls turned in surprise. The temple hall had become full of shadowy figures. Around Gamatea and the silent Urdu gathered more Guardians, male and female. They were forming a circle quietly round the pool.

Gamatea held out her hand to the diminutive Mina. To Sarba's astonishment, Urdu was extending his to her. On her other side, a dark-haired woman was doing the same. These Xerappan Guardians were welcoming her, a Yadu Ring-Holder, into their Circle. Sarba had never willingly touched a Xerappan before. She crossed an enormous divide to take their hands.

She caught the flicker of movement of many jerboas. The distant light of the lamps glistened here and there in round black eyes. There was a deep silence. As their hands joined, no one seemed to feel the need for words. On the summit of Mount Femarrat, there would have been chanting, incantations to sing down the Power. She felt the intensity of the silence here. Power was being appealed to; she was sure of that. But what power? She was sure it was protective: it felt loving. But there was sadness, too, in the dimly seen faces. This love might not be able to save them from suffering, yet it would suffer with them.

She shivered. She wanted to call down fire, to blast their enemies. She could not. On her right side, Urdu's sinewy hand squeezed hers in reassurance. His clasp was dry and cool. She remembered the shock in his face when he learned she was Lord Cozuman's daughter. She felt ashamed.

She tried to put her fears aside and merge her mind into this collective silence. She had been trained in a different temple, with other rites, yet she understood something of the nature of this Circle. She knew she had a part to play.

As she gazed across the pool, the twilight before her eyes seemed to lighten. It was as though she were looking out from the tower again into brilliant sunshine. The dunes which had lain in golden stillness were now alive with movement. A dozen or more camels and riders were charging down the slope towards the oasis.

She gasped, and she was back in the temple hall. She could scarcely see in its shadows. Again, that brief pressure of Urdu's hand round hers.

'Well done. You saw.'

'I... how?' Then she saw the glitter of his jerboa's eyes at her feet. Her own eyes went swiftly up to the Deputy Guardian's. 'I *saw*... through him? Your jerboa?' she whispered.

He nodded, saying nothing. She saw his gaze withdraw from her and focus inwardly again. She did the same.

The Sorcerer Guard had halted where the sand levelled out at the foot of the dunes. Some had dismounted from their camels. Her heart missed a beat. Two of those figures wore not the red tunic and trousers of the Sorcerer Guard, but loose robes. One, she knew, must be Examiner Orzad. It was too far away for Sarba to make out the crimson bands around the skirt of the other, but she knew. It was her worst fear. Hania had come.

She felt the Circle round the pool stir. She had not needed to tell them the dread she was feeling. They had read her thoughts.

All of them watched through the eyes of the jerboas on the tower.

Hania was placing something on the sand. Sarba saw the small block of red Stone she had carried from Mount Femarrat. On top of it, she was placing the copper bowl. It would be only moments now.

She cried out, as if in pain, as the column of flame leaped towards the sky. The Guardians were murmuring rapidly now, prayers Sarba could not understand, but whose plea was clear.

There were more shouts of alarm from the tower roof. Sarba squeezed her eyes shut, but the horrifying picture was in her mind. She could not shut it out.

201

Immense green dragons were emerging from the smoke of the flame. They bent their horned heads towards the oasis and spread gigantic wings. The shadow of their flight darkened the sand.

The Circle broke apart in cries of fear. Rasmullin came leaping down from the tower and rushed out of the temple to organize the city's puny defences. Gamatea was trying to re-form the ring of protection, but Sarba flew up the stairs. She was aware of Mina scrambling after her. She had to find Tekran.

The two girls burst out on to the sunlit roof. They almost collided with Novan, who was rushing after Rasmullin, with Alalia behind him. The two Yadu sorcerers were conferring urgently.

Jentiz was saying, 'Granted, that flame will have restored the power to our own spell-rods, but it's just the two of us against some of the High Sorcerer's most powerful men.'

'And women,' said Sarba behind them.

They turned.

'Sarba, get back,' Tekran said sharply. 'We're prime targets here for those dragons.'

Sarba gasped. Over Tekran's shoulder, the sorcerers' dragons darkened the whole sky. Closer and closer they sped. They were swooping low over the fields surrounding the city. Gusts of fire erupted from their mouths. The searing blasts scorched across the crops, setting corn blazing, blackening fields of lettuces. Palm trees burst into flames.

Mina groaned. 'The farms! How can the city survive without them?'

'Women,' insisted Sarba, grabbing Jentiz's arm. 'You said we were up against the High Sorcerer's most powerful men. You forgot Hania.'

The colonel looked puzzled. 'So? True, she called down the flame, but she has no spell-rod, has she?'

'But don't you see? Without the flame, the sorcerers' spell-rods are almost useless. They can only do small magic, one spell at a time.'

Still Jentiz and Tekran stared at her impatiently.

'Behind you!' yelled Mina.

A gigantic green dragon came rushing towards them. Its belch of fire almost reached the temple peak. The four of them ducked below the parapet.

'We have to put that flame out.' Sarba gulped. A handful of words, which went against everything she had been trained for from childhood. She, who had daily lit the fire of Power, must now extinguish it.

'How?' said Jentiz bitterly. 'Do we ride out on our camels to challenge them? We wouldn't get beyond the city walls before those dragons finished us.'

There was a flutter of little brown wings. From the parapet, two tiny black eyes held Sarba's.

She drew a deep, shaking breath. 'How about something rather smaller than camels? Sparrows, for instance?'

Light suddenly flared in Jentiz's eyes. 'Like the sparrow who brought you the letter?'

'And the sparrow who showed you Vendel's secret,' Tekran added. 'But I still don't see... Disguised as sparrows, we might get near them, but how do we put out the flame?'

'You saw what Vendel did. He reduced his spell-rod to the size of a pin.'

'And once we're there, with our little spell-rods, I could hold the transformation into sparrows, while *you*...!'

Tekran and Jentiz threw each other looks of triumph.

'I think it might work!' Jentiz said.

He raised Vendel's spell-rod. Words poured from his lips. Sarba saw Mina cover her ears. She longed to do the same herself. But she had once been a Ring-Holder. Though she could not comprehend what those words were, she knew what they were meant to do.

She seized Tekran's hand. He looked startled. She thought he was going to forbid her. But it was too late. The words were spoken. The spell was done.

In a rush, the world grew enormously large around her. She was down on the floor at Mina's sandalled feet, balanced on tiny claws. Two other brown sparrows were in front of her. The larger, which she assumed to be Jentiz, looked at her with angry black eyes. He had not intended to take a Ring-Holder with him.

She cocked her head on one side and flexed her wings. She was relieved to see, tucked into his neck feathers, a minute sliver of white. The other sparrow's wing brushed hers. Looking sideways, she caught Tekran's eye. The two of them spread their wings wider. Jentiz followed suit. Mina stepped back to give them room.

It took courage to rise into the brilliant air and fly towards the darkness which was the approaching dragons.

The flame glowed under the shadow of those enormous wings. The knot of sorcerers was gathered around it. There was another figure besides Hania, his robes more red than white. Examiner Orzad. Sarba remembered his genial smile, the way he encouraged you to tell him more than you should. She shivered, even as she flew towards him.

Let us be small enough, brown enough, inconspicuous enough to escape his attention.

Even as she prayed that, she was aware they were not alone. The air was full of sparrows. Her heart lifted with joy as they flocked around the three disguised Yadu. Could even Orzad's sharp mind pick out the two little brown birds with a tiny white pin in their feathers?

The flock swooped down to the foot of the dunes. Sarba dared not turn to see how the dragons themselves might even now be swooping down more terribly on the Forgotten City. Its fate depended now on these sparrows.

From this small height, only a hand's breadth from the ground, the small red Stone looked almost as large as the altar on Mount Femarrat, the little copper bowl as broad. The flame rose tall and shimmering.

Jentiz's beak bent round on to his feathered neck. It pulled the white pin out. Sarba saw Orzad's sandalled foot move forward abruptly.

'Stop them!' he cried. His hand flew to the spell-rod in his girdle.

The air around him was filled with the noisy twitter of sparrows taking flight. Somewhere among it, Sarba hoped, were the words of Jentiz's spell. She rose into the air herself, vainly trying to distinguish Tekran from the others. Flashes of red shot from the Examiner's rod. Heartbroken, Sarba saw several scorched birds drop to the ground. But she scarcely had power to stop and look. The wind was rising. Clouds of sand whirled stingingly into the air. Orzad flung up his arm to protect his face. All the sorcerers were pulling scarves round their heads. Hania was covering hers with a fold of her robe.

Then Sarba saw no more. She was being hurled back towards the Forgotten City, tossed by the gale. In front of her were the dragons. She would be flung straight into their path. Gusts of flame were directed at the city walls. A tree inside them ignited.

As the sandstorm swept her towards the city, the air should have become still darker. Yet, curiously, it was lightening. Close in front of Sarba now was a fearsome dragon. Leathery green wings angled like an enormous bat. Its armoured scales glittered with a thousand pinpoints of fire lit from its jaws. Its talons were hooked, ready to descend on the city and its inhabitants.

All this she saw with despair as the storm swept her towards it. Then she became aware of where the greater light was coming from. The coarse green web of the gigantic wing in front of her was becoming translucent. She was beginning to glimpse blue sky beyond. The wing was disintegrating before her eyes.

The fire from the dragon's jaws was paling. The scales growing dull, insubstantial. Even as she was flung into the space where it had just been, the monster dissolved into nothingness.

She was being stung by sand. The feathers were hardly enough to protect her. She must rest soon, find shelter.

She staggered on a current of air over the city wall. Did she have the strength to reach the pyramid?

She fell, rather than flew down, to land on the temple steps. She was surrounded by exhausted birds. Somewhere among them, she desperately hoped, were Tekran and Jentiz.

Gentle hands were lifting her. How had Gamatea known which, out of all this flock, she was? Then she saw the white jerboa looking up at her in concern. Of course.

'Are you all safe?'

The whisper in her mind startled her so much that she fluttered wildly in Gamatea's hands. Was it possible? Had she, a Yadu, heard a jerboa speak?

'Yes,' said Gamatea, with a hint of a smile in her voice. 'Even the Yadu can, if they will listen.'

'It worked, didn't it?' she gasped, though the sound was no more than a feeble cheep. 'The dragons vanished. Jentiz's sandstorm has put out the flame.'

'Yes, thank the Jerboa. He turned the power they tried to use against us to destroy that power itself.'

But the fear would not go away. 'And the Sorcerer Guard? Hania? ... The Examiner Orzad? Has it destroyed them, too?'

Chapter Twenty

Another sparrow fluttered down beside Gamatea on the temple steps. Sarba caught the little flash of white in its beak.

'Jentiz?' she cheeped.

The sparrow flicked the tiny wand.

The world changed. Sarba felt her body forcing Gamatea's startled hands apart. Her feet were touching the steps. She was standing taller than the Guardian. She was herself again. Beside her stood Tekran, with a full-size spell-rod in his hand. He grinned at her.

'No, it's me. Disappointed?'

'Tekran!' She flung herself into his arms. 'You're safe?' Too late, she remembered the self-control her training had taught her, as she looked up at the laughing young sorcerer so close to her. She flushed violently and tried to regain her dignity. 'And the colonel?'

His face changed. 'I couldn't see. I was swept along in the storm, like you. Speaking of which, we should get under cover.' He pulled her towards the temple door.

But the clouds of stinging sand were thinning. The wind dropped. An eerie calm fell over the oasis.

Sarba tried to shake the sand from her hair. 'Jentiz succeeded, didn't he? He must have. Those dragons vanished.' She was talking fast to cover her confusion.

'The sandstorm smothered the flame. By now, the Stone and the bowl must be buried so deep in the dunes, no one will ever find them again.'

'So the Sorcerer Guard are powerless?'

'I wouldn't say that. Not quite. Jentiz and I can still work a little magic, even without the flame. If they've still got their spell-rods, they're dangerous.'

'What will they do now?'

'They'll be *very* angry.'

Out of the sky came limping a last sparrow, struggling on exhausted wings. It tumbled on to the steps at their feet. Gamatea bent to lift it, but Tekran pointed his spell-rod and spoke a few soft words. Colonel Jentiz stood before them, in his crimson tunic and trousers. His face was haggard.

Tekran moved swiftly to support him.

'Oh, well done!' Sarba hugged Jentiz. 'You saved us from the dragons. You've saved the whole city.'

Gamatea bowed. 'I don't know how to thank you. More than ever, you have proved a friend to the Xerappans. I apologize that our people ever arrested you as a spy.'

He managed a twisted smile. 'I'd have done the same in their place. You have the safety of this city to think of. I'm only sorry I didn't act in time to save your crops from the flames. What will you do now, with no food supply?'

'I can scarcely think about that,' Gamatea sighed. 'We relied on being self-sufficient. And we're not safe yet. These young people tell me that the Sorcerer Guard will still have some magical powers. You trained on Mount Femarrat, like them. You're a high-ranking officer. What would you do now if you were them?'

Jentiz's brow furrowed. He tapped the rod against his palm. 'I think,' he said at last, 'I would realize that I didn't have enough troops to meet you Xerappans head-on. Sorcery could kill or immobilize many, but the Guard could still be overwhelmed by sheer numbers. I'd use guile. I'd do what Tekran and I have just done with us. I'd transform the Sorcerer Guard and their Ring-Holder into a guise which could get past your sentries undetected.'

'Like?'

'Flies, perhaps?'

'And then?'

'I would order my sorcerers to make their way into your headquarters. To seek out the leaders of this city. Then they could shed their disguise and use their sorcery to kill you.'

'Do you think that would quell our Xerappans? Those who were left would elect new leaders. Rasmullin and I are not indispensable.'

'There might be no need for replacements. These sorcerers could transform themselves to look like you.'

Sarba turned as cold as ice. She knew it was possible. She had seen Vendel with the curly black beard of a Xerappan. She had a vision of Hania, standing where Gamatea now stood. Looking like her, with the Guardian's waving black hair and her vivid blue eyes, wearing the same cloak. Would the Ring-Holder do this? Was she as murderous as Colonel Gordoz or Examiner Orzad? Was this what Sarba herself had been trained for?

It wouldn't need to be a woman. Examiner Orzad, now, different from the other sorcerers in his flowing robes. He would impersonate Gamatea very well. The thought was horrifying.

'We're only guessing,' said Tekran. 'They could easily do something we'd never have thought of.'

'Just as important,' said Jentiz to Gamatea, 'what will *you* do?'

'We must save what we can. Rasmullin is already directing gangs to put out the fires. As for me, I shall hold the Circle, to the end.'

She smiled rather sadly at Sarba. The Yadu girl blushed. She remembered how she had broken her hold on Urdu and the Xerappan girl on her left, how she had dashed up the stairs to be with the sorcerers on the tower roof. How she had seized

Tekran's hand, so that she, too, would be transformed into a sparrow and fly to the desert. She had not needed to do that. Jentiz and Tekran could have managed it alone. Without her bracelet, she had no help to give them. She had run away from the only place where she might have done any good.

'It's not too late,' a voice whispered in her mind. *'They still need you at the pool.'*

She looked down. Gamatea's white jerboa was staring at her urgently.

Her eyes were used to the twilight of the temple now. She stood, hands linked with two other Xerappan women, one older, one about her age. The pool shimmered darkly at their feet. It sounded easy, to stand in a circle and give her mind and heart to whatever power of good could help them now.

It was not easy. Her arms ached from holding them extended to her neighbours so long. Her heart was full of fear. The Sorcerer Guard were coming, she knew it. But there was no way of knowing how they would come. The littlest creature, creeping unseen into this shadowy space, could suddenly erupt into a terrifying sorcerer with spell-rod poised to strike. It was only a question of when.

There was another unease she tried to fight down. She was ashamed to confess it now. It was still not easy for her to stand in this ring of Xerappans, holding Xerappan hands. Ever since she could remember, she had recoiled from contact with them. The vision of her mother rose up in front of her. Xerappans had done that. Xerappans had tried to kill little Sarba, too.

'All Xerappans?'

The whisper in her mind startled her. She was not yet used to the realization that the jerboas could speak to her, too. She cast around, trying to locate the source of communication. Mina was there, some way across the pool. Her piebald jerboa was sitting up at her feet. It was too far away to make out the bright black eyes, but its saucer-like ears seemed to be directed at Sarba.

'Look around you. Look at the walls.'

Between the pillars which looked like palm trunks, she caught the occasional gleam where a lamp on the wall shed a golden glow. Now that she stared carefully, she saw the walls were not uniformly dark. They were covered in paintings, their colours glowing where the lamplight fell on them. It was difficult to make out a complete picture. There seemed to be crowds of people, of many nations. Here, turbaned black faces advanced with eager smiles. There, sharper features showed under loose headcloths. There were children with golden curls and dark, slant-eyed women in slender tunics. All seemed to be carrying gifts. They were converging on some scene shown on the distant wall opposite the temple door. It was difficult to focus. The light was faint and far away. There seemed to be two figures, painted larger than all the rest. They were seated. On thrones? A woman and a man. She caught the glint of golden crowns.

She started. She saw the difference between them now. An impossible difference, surely? The woman had long, straight fair hair, just like Sarba's own. The man, a little smaller than her, had cropped black curls. A Yadu queen, with a Xerappan king? Behind the pair rose the unmistakable white cone of Mount Femarrat.

It was a shock, as if someone had punched her in the heart. Her father had always told them that the Yadu had a right to the land which had once been called Xerappo, that they were only taking back what the Xerappans had stolen from them. He had not told them that a Yadu and a Xerappan had ruled side by side, that they were once equal partners in this land.

Suddenly, a truth which had been gnawing at the back of her mind sprang into focus. Gamatea! Why had she felt so safe in the presence of the Chief Guardian? Why had she not recoiled from the touch of Gamatea's hands when they held her as a sparrow? Was it because Gamatea, unusually among these dark-eyed Xerappans, had eyes as blue as the noonday sky? Had something in her recognized that kinship? Was the Guardian descended from that couple on their thrones, part Yadu, part Xerappan?

She drew her eyes back to the Circle. If that were true, now more than ever, she needed to pray, not just for her own safety as a fugitive, and Tekran's, but for the safety of this place, all these people. This time she must mean it with her whole heart.

There was movement in the doorway. She gasped. Two young people were coming into the temple, hand in hand: Alalia Yekhavu, and with her, Novan, the Xerappan she was betrothed to. The resemblance to the picture was overwhelming. The fair-haired Yadu girl, with the sturdy Xerappan young man. The painting was not ancient history, nor a vision of the possible future. These two were making it a reality, here and now.

Were the Xerappans Sarba's people, too?

Tentatively, she made herself press the hands of her neighbours a little more warmly.

'Thank you.'

This time, the whisper in her mind came almost from her feet. The two women's jerboas were just visible in the shadows. A wave of embarrassment swept over her. All the time she had been holding the Xerappans' hands and flinching from contact with them, they had known what she was thinking.

She took a deep breath and tried to still her mind. Prayer required concentration. It was work. She must not be the link which weakened the chain.

She gazed down into the wide, dark circle of the pool. What had Mina said about it? Something strange. That there was a

212

pool like this in the heart of Mount Femarrat. Novan, Mina, Alalia and her brother had gone under its waters to escape her betrothal to Digonez. How could that be possible?

It was too late to ask. Pinpoints of light from the distant lamps danced on the surface. There must be a draught from the door rippling the water. Next moment, too late to cry out a warning, Sarba knew that something else had entered the temple.

She never saw the form it took. Suddenly, terrifyingly tall, the sorcerer was there in their midst. And he was worse than any she had dreaded. Not the sinister Vendel, now a prisoner. Not Colonel Gordoz, to whom her father had entrusted his mission of vengeance. Not the slyly ingratiating Examiner Orzad.

Before her, on the other side of the pool, appeared the furious figure of her cousin Digonez, the man Alalia Yekhavu had refused to marry. The shoulders of his red uniform were straining with his rage.

Alalia screamed. Digonez seized the terrified girl and dragged her towards him. With a shout of protest, the smaller Novan lunged to fight him off.

Digonez raised his white wand.

From behind Sarba came a flash of golden fire. The surface of the pool blazed momentarily. Digonez's hand, which had been holding Alalia, clutched emptiness. Where Novan had stood directly in the path of the sorcerer's slay-spell, there was nothing to be seen. Or almost nothing. Something like two dust motes floated across a ray of sunlight from the open door. They might have been a pair of moths.

Sarba turned. Tekran was standing behind her, his spell-rod levelled towards Digonez. He looked a little startled, even embarrassed.

'It worked! I wasn't sure it would.'

Digonez swung round towards the young sorcerer who had once been his colleague. His face was maddened.

'You traitor!'

Another searing blast of fire shot from his spell-rod. Sarba knew with certainty it must mean the death of Tekran. It would probably kill her too, standing beside him. The ball of flame shot across the pool. Where Tekran's spell had been reflected as gold, this was a dreadful blood red.

A heartbeat later, Sarba realized that she was still watching it. The red fire hung over the centre of the pool.

Digonez uttered some awful words. The fireball quivered, as if struggling to complete its journey.

'Amazing,' said Tekran quietly. 'This time, I didn't do anything.'

The flame sank, down towards the centre of the dark water. There was a fierce hiss. Then nothing. The temple seemed extremely dark.

'It's the pool itself,' said Tekran. 'It swallowed his spell.'

Then Sarba felt a prickle in her spine from behind her. She knew, before she turned, what she would see. And this time, there would be no magic pool between her and them.

Another red sorcerer's uniform: Sergeant Ilian, no longer the friendly camel-driver. And two robed figures which filled her with yet more horror: Examiner Orzad and Hania, with vengeance in their faces.

Orzad levelled his spell-rod at her.

Chapter Twenty-One

Orzad smiled. That smile was as terrifying to Sarba as his spell-rod. She stood frozen in its cold path.

'Sarba, you disappoint us. You will disappoint your father. The High Sorcerer will be most upset to learn about the manner of your death.'

'Traitor!' shouted Hania, losing her usual dignity. 'We trusted you. We should never have given a Two-Ring-Holder such responsibility.'

'Shall I fell her, sir?' Sergeant Ilian's own spell-rod was twitching.

'I think this is a pleasure I shall reserve for myself.'

Orzad's robed arm lifted.

Two things happened simultaneously. Fire flashed from the Examiner's spell-rod. Tekran threw himself in front of Sarba.

Screams echoed round the temple chamber. Sarba did not know if hers was among them. She waited in agony for Tekran's body in front of her to fall.

Instead, all she could see falling to the ground were showers of sparks, like the colourful close to a witch-fire display. They tumbled to meet their reflections on the wet floor.

Wet? What was this coolness around her sandalled feet? She stared more closely. Waves were lapping the edge of the pool and spilling over. They swallowed the fragments of Orzad's felling-spell and left a hushed twilight.

Belatedly, Sarba realized that Tekran was still standing unharmed. She began to shake with relief.

'What happened?' asked Hania nervously. 'Why isn't your magic working? How are they countering it?'

'We're not,' gasped Tekran, recovering himself. 'It's this place.'

Another blast of flame, this time from Ilian. Again, a fountain of yellow sparks fell harmlessly into the ripples.

Sarba looked across the overflowing pool at Gamatea. Her voice echoed strangely from the painted walls. 'Is this the Power you were summoning, when you made your Circle? Did *I* help to summon this? Can it really be more powerful than sorcerers' spells?'

Gamatea's voice sang back to her. 'We do not *summon* the power in the pool. If we could, it would be our tool, less powerful than we are. When we make our Circle, we ask its help and give ourselves into its hands. We offer ourselves, to be used where, and when, and how it needs us, in the cause of good. It may be our living which is needed; it may be our death. It seems that, today, the Good needs your life, not your death.'

Even as she spoke, there was a commotion beside the Chief Guardian. It took a few moments for Sarba to realize with horror what was happening.

'Tekran! Your transformation-spell! It's stopped working!'

The sorcery which had enchanted Alalia and Novan out of reach of Digonez's fury was failing. The fair Yadu girl and the dark Xerappan boy tumbled out of the air in which they had been flying, no longer moths. They landed helplessly beside the High Sorcerer's nephew.

Novan lunged desperately for his adversary. He wrenched Digonez's spell-rod out of his hand and sent it spinning across the floor. Jentiz flew through the doorway, leaping to help him. Digonez lashed out violently, hurling curses at the two of them. There was a whirlwind of red and white as they wrestled.

216

Tekran went sprinting round the pool to help, but Sergeant Ilian blocked his way.

Digonez was down. Novan had a knee on his neck. Jentiz was trying to use his spell-rod to hold him.

Noise from outside shattered Sarba's momentary relief. There were shouts, screams coming from the city. Whatever salvation there was in this temple, awful violence was happening out there. She licked her dry lips. Was it only their closeness to the pool which was saving them?

Sarba measured the distance between herself and Tekran and the two sorcerers and Hania confronting them. If spells failed, it would come down to brute force. She had no doubt that Sergeant Ilian would be a formidable opponent with his bare hands. Then she remembered the knife every sorcerer carried, and shuddered.

She saw Orzad's eyes signal to Hania. The Examiner and the Ring-Holder began to move. Sergeant Ilian took a purposeful step closer.

Sarba caught a movement in the shadows. Some of the Guardians were beginning to creep round behind them. Something in her eyes must have warned Hania. The older woman turned.

Tekran leaped for Orzad's spell rod.

At the same moment, on the far side of the water, Digonez broke free from his captors and sprang to seize Alalia. The furious sorcerer towered over the girl.

A slight figure in a dark red dress moved swiftly. Mina's push caught Digonez off balance. His boots skidded on the wet tiles. His arms flailed wildly. With an oath, he somersaulted backwards and hit the pool with a resounding splash.

What happened next, Sarba could never afterwards recall with certainty. Imprinted on her memory was the vision of a fountain erupting from the pool. White water grew taller and taller, until it reared over them like an upside-down image of Mount Femarrat's cone. Still higher and wider it rose, until its bubbling canopy overspread the whole pool. Sarba stood rooted to the spot in awe, oblivious of her danger.

When it had almost reached the far roof of the temple, the tower of water broke. A deluge descended, drenching her, robbing her of breath and sight and hearing.

It seemed a long while before she came to her senses again. She shook herself, feeling she must be waking from an impossible dream. She found, astonishingly, that she was still standing in the temple. Tekran, equally surprised, was grasping Orzad's lifted arm. They were all soaked through.

'Where's it gone? What have you done with my spell-rod?' Sergeant Ilian's shout brought her eyes to him. He was frantically searching in the water swilling over the floor, as the tidal wave poured back into the quaking pool.

She looked back at Orzad. Her fear escaped her in a long gasp. His hands were empty too. Only Hania stood nursing her Ring-Holder's bracelet with her other hand, as if afraid to let it go.

'The pool has taken it,' said Sarba to Ilian, knowing with certainty it was true.

'And mine, too,' whispered Tekran.

The sorcerers stared down into the water. Just faintly, they could all see luminous wands of white slipping very slowly deeper and deeper under the surface.

'Does that mean I'll never get it back?' said Tekran.

Nobody answered.

Mina's voice cried out, shrill with shock and guilt. 'Digonez! What's happened to him?'

Only then did Sarba remember those frantic moments of struggle on the far side of the pool, before the water erupted. Mina and Alalia and Novan were crowding at the edge of the pool, staring down, as she and Tekran were on this side.

Mina's hand was over her mouth.

'What have I done? Isn't he going to come to the surface?'

Alalia put an arm round her. 'We don't know what's happened to him. You and I and Novan and Balgo went under the pool in Mount Femarrat, didn't we? And we came out on the other side. Maybe there's a way out for Digonez, too.'

'Do you want that? After all he's done to us?' Novan asked.

Alalia looked at him in silence. Novan flushed.

'I know. There's been enough killing on both sides.'

She squeezed his hand.

The stillness of wonder in the dim space was shattered as the door crashed open, letting in a flood of light and noise. Tekran let go of Orzad, and whirled round, his empty hands raised in defence.

Rasmullin, Defender of the City, burst in, with twenty or so of his fighters behind him. Regardless of the danger of slay-spells, they flung themselves on the Examiner and Sergeant Ilian, and, more reluctantly, on Hania. Tekran leaped to help them. Sarba grabbed hold of Hania's bracelet arm.

Orzad and Ilian had their knives out now. There was a wild, bloody tussle. Without sorcery it could only end one way. The Xerappans far outnumbered the invaders. Ilian, Orzad and Hania were overpowered. It took several moments more before the Xerappans realized that their captives held no magical weapons.

It was shocking to Sarba to see the men and woman she had been so in awe of made prisoners and to know that she had helped to do this.

Rasmullin laughed breathlessly. 'So, for once, power wasn't all on one side.'

It was only then that Sarba saw the bloody slash on Tekran's arm. She ran to him, tearing a strip from her dress to bandage it. His blood streaked her hands.

'Ouch!' he said through white lips. 'Thank you.'

She put her arm round him to steady him.

The three captives were led away past them, their arms bound.

At the door, Sergeant Ilian twisted his head back to appeal to Sarba. 'What happened to Amber, miss? I couldn't understand why Major Vendel wanted him, out of all the camels in the line. Is he all right?'

She tried to keep her voice level. 'Yes, he's fine. Vendel chose him as the sort of ordinary camel no one would recognize. But he's the only one I've ever ridden. I'd know those eyelashes anywhere.'

'That's something, anyway. It's always the camels I worry about.'

'More than people?' she said softly. But he was gone.

'Is everyone safe?' Rasmullin called to Gamatea. His eyes penetrated into the deeper shadows beyond the door. 'Why are all of you dripping wet?'

Gamatea gave a shaky little laugh. 'Safe? No one who serves the Good is safe. But today, the pool saved us. The only one lost is the High Sorcerer's nephew. The water took him.'

Rasmullin stared down into the quivering pulses of ripples. 'Drowned?'

'Who knows?' Gamatea raised her eyes to gaze, not at Rasmullin, but across at Sarba. 'Legend says that there is a link between this pool and the one under Mount Femarrat.'

'Between here and... home?'

Xerappan heads flew up at her last word. She knew too late that she had reminded them of the bitter truth.

'Yes,' said Gamatea softly. 'You are still the High Sorcerer's daughter.'

'I can't help it. He sent me away. He doesn't love me.'

Tekran moved beside her. His good arm went round her shoulders.

'Lord Cozuman has been deeply hurt, as we all have.'

Gamatea's voice steadied. 'That is why I took such a risk to bring you here. The sorcerers have to give up their power, not only here, but on Mount Femarrat. We can never defeat your father, so he has to change, and someone has to make him want to.' Her gaze held Sarba's.

She felt Tekran squeeze her shoulders.

'Yes,' she whispered, with a gulp of breath. 'That's what has to happen, isn't it?'

There was silence.

Or almost silence. As their voices died, Sarba was aware that the air was full of a tiny squeaking. One by one, the others realized it too.

'The jerboas!' Novan cried.

Mina gasped, 'We never thought! Oh, my stars, what's happened to them? They must have been washed away when the pool erupted!'

They all rushed to peer into the water.

Multiple flecks of golden light flickered in the eddies around the pool. The water was full of tiny heads riding the ripples. Sparks glinted in their luminous, dark eyes. Novan and Mina were down on their knees, scooping the jerboas out with their hands. Others were bending to help them. Soon the floor was alive with tiny desert rats, twitching drops from their fur, grooming their whiskers, shaking their spoon-shaped ears.

A bedraggled Thoughtcatcher glared up at Mina. *All your lives, we've given you warning of danger. Next time you're going to raise a tidal wave, you might at least tell us.'*

But the air above, too, was full of cheeping. The sunlight of the doorway darkened momentarily as a flock of sparrows burst in. They circled round the pool, so that the whole temple was alive with their wings. A crown of tiny brown birds danced around Sarba and Tekran's heads. One settled jubilantly on her outstretched hand. As its feathers brushed her skin, she saw the black cap and bib, and her heart caught with joy. She was almost sure she recognized the bright friendship of those black eyes.

All Lion books are available from your local bookshop, or can be ordered via our website or from Marston Book Services. For a free catalogue, showing the complete list of titles available, please contact:

Customer Services
Marston Book Services
PO Box 269
Abingdon
Oxon
OX14 4YN

Tel: 01235 465500
Fax: 01235 465555

Our website can be found at:
www.lionhudson.com

If you want to know more about
Fay Sampson's books, see her website:
www.faysampson.co.uk